Grandmother's Ghost

Janet Kay Gallagher

Publishing Coordinator – Sharon Kizziah-Holmes

WINTER LAKE
P R E S S

ISBN -13: 978-1-951772-08-6

Dedication

To my wonderful son Ken,
who encouraged me and pushed me to write and
finish my stories.

Acknowledgments

In 2009 I attended a writing group led by Nicholas Inman. When he got a full-time job at the Marshfield Mail Newspaper, he asked me to take over the group and keep it going. I have been leading that group and in 2019 we celebrated our 10-year Anniversary. Our current name is *The Quill and Ink Writers*. Special thanks to current members, Myrtle DeLaney, Mitch DeLaney, Ruby Joyce, Anita Keeling, Claudette Smith, Carolyn Moye, Betty Jo Cantrell, and Melissa Mall. I am thankful for all who have attended over the years and listened to my stories and given feedback. Special Remembrance of Charles Christman, and Elsie Myers who was an original member we lost last year.

I needed to learn about writing so I attended a book signing in Springfield, Missouri that was associated with the 2009 *ORA Writers Conference*. I met the authors who were speaking at the conference. And best yet I met members of the local writing groups, *Ozarks Romance Authors (ORA), Sleuths' Ink Mystery Writers, Ozarks Writers League and Springfield Writers Guild*.

I was so impressed with the people I met that day, that I joined all the groups.

I met Cait London, one of my long-time favorite authors, who lived in Branson and belonged to *ORA*. Sharon Kizziah-Holmes who is my publisher/encourager. Shirley McCann smiles and brightens the world. She told me to, write, edit, submit and do it again. Barbara Bettis, Nancy Dailey, V.J. Schultz, Ruth Hunter, Rose Lombardo, and I know I have left out some. I want everyone in these groups to know I am glad to call you friend and that each of you has played a part in my writing success.

Special Thanks to Susan Keene and Tierney James who take me to Springfield Writers meetings with them. You have shared friendship, knowledge and encouragement with me.

You will find wonderful hours of reading enjoyment by checking out the names listed on this page as they are authors to add to your: TO READ LIST.

Chapter 1

or several days Eva and her housekeeper Katherine quietly searched everywhere they could think of where Eva might have lost the Amulet of Safety. They had hoped no one would find out it was gone. They sat in the library in front of a blazing fire while they discussed what action to take.

"Eva how could you forget to wear the amulet for over a month?" Katherine asked.

"Katherine, how can I tell Mother the Amulet of Safety is lost, because I've been careless. When Grandmother gave it to me, she put special protection spells on it for my safety. Since the amber necklace is so well known and valuable and not suitable to wear for every occasion, I always needed to keep it on my person in the special pocket that looked like an envelope. A large button sewn on the petticoats held it securely. All three of the buttonholes in the pocket back, front and closed flap kept it safe."

"I don't know when it went missing. It must have been before William went off in one of his snits." Eva said.

"When I realized it wasn't among my belongings, I asked you, to help me find it, with no results. It looks like Amber Manor will have to be searched from top to bottom. It will take days.

We will need to involve the entire staff. I would hate for them to know their mistress, Eva Smythe Davis, is so thoughtless that she lost, misplaced or allowed to be stolen such a valuable piece of jewelry."

The young women talked a long time before they came up with a plan. They hoped it would work as they couldn't think of another way to obtain the information. They were sure someone must know what happened to the necklace.

They decided Eva would accuse Katherine of taking it. She would do this in front of one of the maids, Ellen, who was known as the gossip of Amber Manor. Their play acting would spread like wildfire through the house. If any of the household staff knew anything about it, they would surely come forward. Eva and Katherine needed their plan to work and the amulet to be found.

The next morning, Eva stood at the doorway and tapped her foot as she waited for Ellen, who had brought the tea service earlier and would be back to pick it up soon.

Eva heard footsteps. She turned to Katherine and

whispered the signal for their plan to begin, "She's coming."

"Katherine, my necklace is missing. Return the Amulet of Safety by Friday or else I will notify the constable!" Eva screamed. She pivoted toward the door, her long deep blue taffeta skirts swirled. The fancy white lace ruffle edging the skirt whipped around her ankles as she stalked out of the room. As planned, Katherine stared after Eva, acting thunderstruck.

Sarah, Eva's mother, was seated in one of the burgundy leather chairs placed on either side of the fireplace. She looked small sitting there knitting one of her famous scarves for charity. Her dark brown hair showed no signs of gray. She had aged well and was considered a beauty. She watched as Eva made her dramatic exit.

Katherine turned toward Sarah and said, "Why would Eva accuse me of taking the necklace? She must know I would never take anything from her. Especially something as valuable as the gold and amber amulet her grandmother gave her. It's said that she put spells on it to protect Eva."

Katherine twisted a handkerchief in her hand. "The amulet is so well known in these parts I doubt anyone could possibly sell it. Everyone believes its bewitched. Most people would be afraid to touch it for fear a curse would come on them. Some of the help are afraid to even look upon it."

Ellen entered the room, retrieved the tea cart and quietly left. Katherine was sure she'd overheard the entire conversation. She could see part of Ellen's starched black uniform skirt that didn't clear the door frame. She knew Ellen hadn't moved far from the door. The manor's gossip was on duty.

Katherine looked down toward her feet and said. "I don't understand how Eva could misjudge me so cruelly. Mrs. Smythe, you must know I had no part in the amulet's disappearance." A tear slid down her cheek and fell to the floor.

Sarah said "No need to cry dear, you were born at Amber Manor and I have known you all your life. I knew your parents. Katherine, I trust you. Where Eva came up with the idea that you took her necklace is beyond me. This matter will work itself out. The amulet is insured and the portrait of Mary Beth, in the gallery, depicts it very well. It would be hard to hide. Look for it, perhaps it fell under the bed, dresser or a chair."

Sarah dropped a stitch and made the correction in her knitting. "You are an excellent housekeeper and I'm sure you'll find it, Eva walked the grounds yesterday, she could have lost it anywhere. Let me know when you find it." She gave the young woman a gracious and encouraging smile.

Ellen had left the hall sometime before Katherine, left the morning room. She stood in the doorway and admired its spacious floor to ceiling arched windows and light sunshine-yellow walls. A large mahogany desk and matching chair and the writing implements, that always fascinated her, stood in front of the mahogany bookshelves. The bookcases had an ornate scroll design like the desk and chair.

She was grateful Sarah allowed her to use the room in the evenings to write at the desk.

Sometimes she would sit in the huge rose-colored wing-back chair with her feet on the ottoman and read. The ornate bookshelves called her name. As an avid reader she could imagine a book heroine in a similar situation.

What would the book character do now? She would make a plan and follow it.

With their plan in motion the next step was to search the house with all the servants and look for the precious amulet. They hoped one of the staff would know where to find it.

Would any of the staff know someone who can dispose of illicit goods? If so maybe one of the maids might know what happened to the necklace and will come forward.

When Katherine gathered everyone and told them of the missing amulet, and they would all be needed to search for it, most of them had already heard about the lost necklace. Their plan had worked so far.

By nightfall Katherine and all the household maids had searched first Eva's room then the other twenty-nine bedrooms in this wing, and all the servants quarters. Each room was checked off the housekeeper's list after it was gone over completely. Progress was slow but thorough.

Exhausted Katherine fell across her bed with her clothes on and pulled her warm pink quilt over her.

Eva's dead grandmother stood at the end of Katherine's bed. "Come with me," the ghost ordered.

Katherine was startled. Her heart, beat so fast it might cause a heart attack or a stroke, but she said aloud. "Is this a dream? Am I still asleep? You are dead. Are you a specter? Ghosts aren't real; are they? I see your face and yet I can see through you." She wanted to go back to sleep and dismiss this apparition. Goosebumps formed on her arms. It had to be fear and maybe shock. She was very cold.

The ghost of Mary Beth Hamilton Smythe said in her no-nonsense voice, "Katherine, I'm here, and yet I'm dead, so I must be a ghost. Get up! We'll go to Eva and find the Amulet of Safety."

Katherine said, "Thank God you know I didn't take it. We were only play acting."

Mary Beth said, "Of course, I know you did no such thing. Let's go."

Katherine got out of bed, but her feet weren't on the floor. They both hovered above it. As Mary Beth took her hand, she opened her eyes wide, she didn't want to miss anything, as the old lady's ghost guided her through several walls to Eva's room.

The Housekeeper looked at the ghost. "What a way to travel. This is amazing!"

"Indeed, it's a miracle. Eva's sleeping soundly. Shake her and wake her up."

Katherine shook Eva's arm. It startled her awake, "What are you doing in my room?"

"I'm here to wake you so we can go with your grandmother and retrieve the necklace."

Katherine had shaken her with more force than necessary but the events that brought her to Eva's room had unnerved her. A ghost who moved you through space was not your normal nightly occurrence.

Eva saw her grandmother, screamed, and pointed

as she backed up against the headboard.

"Grandmother, what are you doing here? Did Katherine tell you the amulet is missing? How can Katherine talk to you? Why are you transparent? I can see right through you. Yet you look the same as I remember. Why are you a ghost instead of resting with Jesus?"

Her grandmother held up her finger calling for silence. "Calm down. Get up now and come with me."

Eva obeyed and Mary Beth moved between the girls and held their arms. With ease they moved through the manor, through wood and brick walls. They floated above the ground and with the breeze created by their movement their hair billowed out behind them. It was chilly outside. Mary Beth took them into the stable, and into the tack room.

She said, "Katherine, look behind those boxes in the back and you will find a can with old nails. The amulet is inside."

She did as she was told. Many boxes and old tools had to be moved out of her way before she found the can with old rusty nails. She gently shook the nails out of the can and found a black velvet pouch under them. Katherine was careful dusting it off before she handed it to her mistress, Eva. She returned the nails to the can and put it back in place and made the area look like it did when they started their search for the can.

"Eva, at least it's still in the protective velvet pouch you always keep it in," Katherine said.

Grandmother hugged her. "Eva, you must not be careless. The Amulet of Safety is just that, it is for your protection. It was taken so you could be harmed. I don't know where or when the danger will come. You must always keep it with you, it's imperative that you never forget it. Do you have a pocket in your nightdress?"

Eva said, "Yes, look! The necklace is safe, the glass isn't broken or anything." She took the amulet she had taken out of the velvet, eased it back into the pouch and slipped it into her pocket.

Grandmother nodded her approval. "No one must know it has been found. This is very important. Eva wear it always. Katherine, keep up your search of the house and grounds with the maids tomorrow, so no one knows it has been found. I love you girls."

The ghost of Mary Beth Hamilton Smythe disappeared before their eyes. She dissipated into thin air. The girls began to giggle. Did they have the same dream? They hugged one another and knew for sure it was real. Eva held the amulet in her nightgown pocket. It would go into the button envelope pocket as soon as she got to her bedroom. The two walked arm and arm back to the house. The dew on the grass was wet and cold on their bare feet, and they wished they hadn't forgotten to put on shoes when they traveled through the air with grandmother's ghost.

Katherine turned toward Eva, "What a sensation. We flew above the ground and went through walls. Your grandmother took us to the missing amulet. Yet we can't ever tell anyone, or they might lock us up thinking that we were crazy. I was so scared I thought I'd die of a heart attack upon seeing her ghost at the foot of my bed and realized it was your grandmother."

Eva put a hand to her mouth when she yawned, "Me too. I'm surprised my scream didn't wake everyone in the house. Who took the necklace and why would anyone want to harm me? Grandmother says I'm in danger. I had no time to thank her for showing us where the Amulet was hidden."

Eva was too wound up to go back to sleep. "The night is beautiful. Look at the sliver of a moon. I always enjoy the walk between the stable and the house. It sure didn't take long, lifted and flying with grandmother. Too bad it will have to stay locked in our hearts. Such a nice memory to keep as our special secret. I'm getting cold, let's go to the kitchen and make hot chocolate and see if there is any of that pie left that Martha served at supper tonight."

They continued toward the house. "Katherine, after you search the house and grounds tomorrow, we should argue again in front of one of the servants. Someone must know who hid the amulet. You say something like, 'If you think I took the amulet, send for the constable.' Mother will try to stop me, and I'll agree to her wishes. Perhaps someone will come forward with who hid it and why. Ellen sure got the word out fast. I think it will be worth another try. We should act aloof to each other for a few days then make up our old friendship. Do you agree?"

Katherine looked at her friend. "I talked to the maids as we searched today, and no one indicated they knew anything. But we can try again. It might work, I don't think anyone will come forward since they didn't when we acted out the first time. I'm surprised your Grandmother didn't know who took the amulet, but she knew where to find it. She thought it was important no one know you have it back. We had better do as she said. Do you think she is your guardian angel? I never believed in ghosts, but now I do. I told her she was dead, and ghosts aren't real." She said in her practical tone, "Katherine, you know I'm dead and that I am here, so I must be a ghost. Get Up!"

Eva gave a nervous laugh, as they entered the kitchen door. "What a night."

Katherine splashed some of the Cocoa she was pouring into a cup as Martha the cook came into the kitchen. She picked up a kitchen towel and wiped the counter. "Martha you startled me."

Eva had begun to eat her piece of pumpkin pie but looked up at Martha and smiled with her mouth full and waved her fork at her.

"I heard you and had to see for myself. The two of you invading my kitchen in the middle of the night again. It has been awhile since you have done it. I'm happy to see you here. I was worried with all the goings on and the whole house upset over the missing necklace. Katherine, is there enough hot chocolate and pie for me?"

"There is plenty." She poured another cup of cocoa and cut a piece of pie, put it on a plate with a fork and sat it on the table beside Martha.

Eva swallowed. "Katherine came and begged me to reconsider. We made a truce. I think it was you that told us, 'Food is good to patch up a friendship.'

I must have the amulet back. Katherine and the maids will continue to search for it."

Martha shook her finger at them, "I've watched you grow up together. You need to work this problem out. Friends are for a lifetime. Don't let yourselves become hardened over this loss. A necklace is just an expensive piece of jewelry, no matter how pretty. I hope you find it. Thank you, Katherine, for fixing the cocoa and pie for me. I'll take it back to my room. Good night." She picked up the cup and dessert dish and left.

Eva and Katherine were silent as they ate and drank while they considered the events of the night. When they finished, Katherine washed the dishes in the sink. "We need to get some sleep. Tomorrow will be a long day as we search for the lost amulet. Goodnight, Eva."

"Goodnight, my friend."

While Katherine and the maids searched more of the rooms in the huge mansion, Sarah Smythe sent for the Property Manager, Joseph, and asked him and his men to search the grounds, stables and all the other outbuildings. It was a long hard day for all the workers, and they were exhausted. Of course, they found no amulet.

After supper, Sarah met with Eva and Katherine in the study as usual. It was a comfortable room, decorated in shades of blue, and was filled with books. It also served as the business office for the manor and all their properties.

Ellen, the maid brought in a silver coffee service for their after-supper coffee, Sarah poured it and served the coffee. "I have already been told no one found the Amulet of Safety. Eva I am worried that it is missing. Your Grandmother put special protection spells on it just for you. She thought it was necessary because she felt you would need them. It was first created, and safety spells were put on it for your grandmother. It protected her on several occasions. I'm not going to take time now to tell the stories. They were quite miraculous. She attributed the power that saved her to the amulet."

Eva's brow twitched. She wanted to tell her mother the amulet was back in her secret pocket and that grandmother's ghost visited last night, but she had told Eva not to tell anyone.

Katherine took a sip of her coffee. "Mrs. Smythe, thank you for having Joseph and his men search outside. It was a great help to me. We didn't get the whole house inspected. We will need to resume the search tomorrow. I think we can finish it by evening."

When Eva heard the maid coming to clear the tray, she winked at Katherine. "Mother, I sure hope if anyone knows about the amulets whereabouts they will let us know. I need it to be found. We, searched thoroughly so maybe it was a professional thief who took it, but I haven't heard of any strangers around here."

Katherine stood up. "I'll be in my room. At least, I hope you don't still think I had anything to do with its disappearance. Good night." She ran into the maid on her way out of the study.

She looked back and caught Eva's eye and was sure the servant had heard it all. By the next day everyone on the property and the village would have heard about it.

Sarah was so caught up in the exchange between her daughter and the housekeeper that she hadn't been aware the maid entered as she spoke, "Eva, I'll not have you treating Katherine so badly. Yesterday's tirade was too much. Send for the constable indeed. Where did such an idea come from? Katherine has been a faithful servant as well as your friend and you have wronged her. You will have to consider the amulet lost to us. We must continue our lives as before this tragedy happened."

"Yes, Mother, you're correct. I'm sorry. This has been very upsetting for me."

Ellen retrieved the coffee service and left.

Chapter 2

Two weeks later, life had returned to normal at the Manor. No one on the estate reacted to the amulet drama Eva and Katherine had played out, and they were disappointed.

Eva had been busy getting mission boxes filled and ready to be sent to the church. Several maids, as well as Katherine, Sarah and Eva, had all been knitting for the project. They hoped the people who received the gifts would be happy to have a warm hat, scarf and gloves.

Ellen found Eva in the drawing room. "Mr. Davis is on his way. He sent a runner from the Dove and Cork. He will be home in about two hours. Miss Eva, he wants you to wear the red satin dress and red slippers, with your hair down loose. He requests you wear the Heliotrope perfume he brought you last time he came home."

"Thank you, Ellen." Eva shuddered, as the maid left.

Since the amulet rested in her pocket once again, life had been calm and bright. Her days were filled with riding her beloved horse, Candy, writing letters, knitting lap blankets, and hat, scarf and glove sets, for the church missions' charity.

Her husband William, would be there soon after a stop at the local pub. The smell of stale ale sickened her. Everyone there would know what he wanted from her by the message he told the young runner to deliver.

How dare he ask her to dress in the whore's clothes and wear that perfume. She had no intention of following his orders. William could go back wherever he'd been for the last month. *He's been gone this long and expects me to welcome him back like a loving wife who holds out my arms for his embrace. I won't do it.*

Eva stood, stamped her feet, and went to look for her mother. She located her in the formal dining room working on a large colorful multi-flower arrangement. "William is on his way home. He'll be here in a couple of hours. He sent a runner to let us know."

Sarah covered her look of distress quickly in hopes her daughter didn't see it. She tried to be nice. But William never grew up. "Did you want the cook to make something special for dinner?"

"No whatever we have will be fine." Eva started to put white, yellow, burgundy, and orange mums and bells of Ireland and other beautiful flowers from their garden in one of the large ornate vases.

She told her mother, "I finished packing the mission boxes, there are five of them. Pastor Embers will send them to the Missionaries, Charles and Molly Pearson, who work with the poor and they will be able to help many people have a warmer winter this year. I think we all enjoyed the knitting it is soothing to the mind and a good thing to make time go fast."

The butler opened the massive carved wooden door and let William in. He found Eva and her mother busy with the array of flowers. He stepped up to Eva and kissed her on the cheek. He ran his hand down to her waist and backside. "Why are you wearing that plain everyday gown? I sent a message for you to put on the shiny red dress for my homecoming."

Flower arranging could ruin the dress if water splashed it or a rose thorn could snag the delicate material finish. Supper will be ready in thirty minutes. How was your trip? Did you visit your parents?"

"Hello Sarah." He nodded at Eva's mother. "I already had dinner. Come upstairs with me, Eva. I want to talk to you."

"William, I'm famished, I'll be up after dinner, at my usual time. You must be tired from your travels. Rest, get some sleep, we can talk tomorrow."

"I want to hear all about what has been going on here while I was away. Come up."

"Since you're not tired, we can talk over dinner. Mother and I can eat, and you can listen."

"The men at the pub told everyone, there was

scandal in my home while I was away. I told you to get rid of Katherine. Now look what she has done. She stole your expensive bauble. You should have let me sell it. At least we would have had something to show for it."

Sarah felt her face flush hot. "You wanted to sell Eva's amulet? When was that? Is that where it went?"

William put both hands on his hips. "No, I heard Katherine stole it. How much will the insurance company pay?"

Eva turned toward him. "William, we won't turn in a claim. I hope to find it. We searched the house and grounds. Maybe I lost it while out riding. It will turn up. The constable notified all the towns around us, everyone's watching out for anyone who tries to sell it. If the amulet were stolen by a professional thief, they would know how to sell it. The insurance won't pay on it until all avenues to find the culprit are thoroughly exhausted. There's no need to make a claim now."

Ellen came in and announced supper was ready.

Sarah and Eva left their flowers on the dining room sideboard and took a seat at the large table next to them.

William didn't hold their chairs as a gentleman would have done. He seated himself, then promptly passed out and slid out of the chair onto the floor.

Sarah told the server to take their food to the small dining room. It was elegant but cozy, with the burgundy and cream wide striped silk chair seats and draperies. Sarah loved the apricot colored wall coverings that helped keep the room warm. The ladies shared their meal in peace. That night both women locked their bedroom doors. The housekeeper and Eva's friend Katherine slept in an alcove off Eva's room.

Before they could sleep Eva had to apologized to Katherine. "I am so sorry I insisted we do the play acting. It didn't work and now I have ruined your good name and reputation. I expected someone to know where the amulet went and that they would come forward and tell us. Mother was correct when she told me I wronged you. Please forgive me and continue to be my friend." She hugged her friend and Katherine forgave her.

After waking up on the dining room floor, William washed and dressed before seeking out his wife. A sober, calm man presented himself. He apologized repeatedly. William was nice to be around when he wanted to be. His charm and good looks won out once again and Eva forgave him.

As he had many times before, he again asked her to invite her friends in the ton society to a party at Amber Manor. Eva put him off and mentioned they might do that in the future. She didn't want to tell him he had offended several of her friends at their wedding and another time at a party they attended at Morrison Hall in London and he wasn't welcome among them.

A lifetime friend, Marion Taylor, told her there was gossip, people saying William was a social climber and he said inappropriate things.

Once Marion held a gathering and didn't invite William. However, Eva and her mother were expected to attend. Eva made her excuses, saying she was ill and insisted her mother go, attended by her personal maid. After several days of secret preparation, Sarah and her maid set off in the coach. Sarah stayed several days in London and visited friends.

When William got home from his day at the pub and found out Sarah had gone to the posh Taylor Ball being held at Mallory Manor and Eva hadn't even told him about it, he was furious, and left for a week.

Since then Eva turned down many invitations and never let William know about them. Several times her mother attended events and Eva told him they were not invited.

Since waking in the dining room, William was cordial and tried his best to please his wife with little niceties, a rose on her pillow, rubbing her feet, and he brought sweet treats, like candied figs and dates.

They rode horses together. Martha made picnic baskets each day. They would sit on a blanket under a tree. Life was good. The land was lush with trees and flowers. The blue skies and white clouds made Eva's heart soar. When William acted like a loving husband, she forgot his arrogant attitudes and mean words. Today they planned a leisurely trip to Italy and France and discussed all they would see when they arrived, and places people had told them about, but they had never been. This was a delightful time of dreams and plans and good food and enjoyable surroundings.

He gently leaned her against a tree. "Kiss me like you love me." They hadn't been this romantic in a long time, she knew he loved her. Everything was perfect. William kissed her again. "Let's go home for more of this."

Eva smiled and laughed. Her long wavy blonde hair flowed behind her as they raced back to the stable. She giggled on those times she came in first. She was in the lead when William caught up to her. He rode up so close the horses could easily collide.

She saw his grin, and his eyes shone with a maniacal gleam as he held the reins in his teeth. With both hands William pushed her with all his might. He shoved her right out of her saddle.

Eva fell over Candy's side knowing she would die.

To hit the ground from this pace would break her neck. She saw her long riding skirt was tangled in the stirrup. The horse would drag her after she hit the hard ground. It will be fast. How much pain?

In an instant, all these thoughts changed. Giant hands lifted her by the waist and set her solidly back into her saddle. The giant hands held her a moment as calm, healing power flowed through her body. Eva wanted the feeling to go on forever. Her horse stopped. The giant had saved her. Did she dream it? Was he an Angel? He soothed her even more by the glorious tune he hummed—and then he was gone. It had all happened in mere seconds.

Eva looked around, stunned, as her Grandmother's ghost stepped in front of William. He screamed a high-pitched unearthly sound. His horse reared, tossing William into a huge oak tree. The thud was deafening. By the angle of his body,

Eva could tell he had died on impact.

Her grandmother vanished before Eva could say anything to her. Eva began to cry. She paced her panicked horse, as it took off running when she was startled by William's scream. She returned her to a walk again.

After the fright of the incident wore off a bit, Eva turned back to where the body of her husband lay sprawled against the tree. Blood lay all around him and covered his face. His eyes were wide open, and his lips still spread with his now silent scream.

No one should have had to see such a sight. Yet she couldn't turn away and stared in horrified curiosity.

She dismounted and tied her horse to a branch of a nearby tree. She went back and sat beside William's death tree. Eva looked out the way he faced.

William's spooked horse kept running as if lightning followed him. He was headed back to the stable. The farm hands would see him and come to search for them.

William tried to kill her. Kill her! He wanted to murder his wife. The look in his crazy eyes when he pushed her was one of triumph. They made love and she thought all was going to be well. But he wanted her dead. She would be dead on the cold ground right now if it hadn't been for the giant angel who saved her. Had the Amulet called him to her?

She sat on the cold ground, so different from the heat of the sunshine earlier as they rode. The words, "William tried to kill me," would never pass her lips as she told about his accident. To be a young widow would be bad. A widow who had her husband try to kill her, not at all tolerable. She would tell Mother and Katherine, but no one else could know. It was too horrible for her to comprehend.

A few tears fell for what might have been; should have been. But the reality was relief, not grief. How could the man who promised to cherish and protect, try to kill me? Overwhelming anger flooded her whole being. *Why didn't I see it?*

Chapter 3

*T*here were signs. Eva's lifelong friend, Jane Garver, came to visit and told her about her cousin Pearl Garver's behavior. How she'd acted so badly with William. Pearl had told her cousin, Jane, "I don't care about his marriage. William told me he would marry me soon."

Jane and I thought divorce was his plan. Scandalous as it would have been, neither of us thought William could murder me.

"Murderer, Murderer!" Eva screamed out loud, not sure how long the words had repeated in her mind after the noise ended. She closed her eyes and told herself to calm down. It would be hard keeping William's despicable actions secret. She would have been dead if Grandmother's ghost hadn't guided her and Katherine to find the Amulet of Safety.

Thank God her good friend Katherine reminded her constantly to be sure she still wore the amulet. Otherwise, she would now lie on the cold hard ground with a broken neck.

It was a beautiful day when they started on their regular ride and race across the vast lands of the property. Riding was one of their favorite things to do. They always raced back. Eva usually won. Sometimes they would take a picnic lunch the cook prepared and spread out her favorite blue blanket and enjoy the stream and little pond. She could smell the wildflowers in the fields, the forest area was always cool and lovely. God put so much wonder and beauty in her life, her blessings changed daily. She loved nature and when she was immersed in it, life was grand.

She realized she was cold, clear to the bone. The sun didn't shine as bright and warm, as earlier. Could evil take away the warmth of the sun?

She thought about how she met William.

I first saw William at a debutante ball, as I danced in my white chiffon gown. The crinolines and fluffy skirt flowed with elegance. The seamstress sewed pearls in the shape of roses on the shoulder where a pin would have been worn. My long sleeves belled at the wrist. My satin slippers had seed pearl roses on the top. It was a night filled with delight.

He stood in front of me. "I'm William Dean Davis. And I know you're Lady Eva Julia Smythe. You look ravishing tonight. All the women must be jealous that you found the perfect seamstress, to bring out your natural beauty."

Although she had been schooled in the actions of a lady, she blushed and became flustered. "Why, thank you kind sir."

William filled in three spaces on her dance card. He held her close while they danced. The feelings he generated in her were forbidden. She needed to control herself no matter how strong her feelings were. Nothing had prepared her for her flushed face, heat and tingling when he spoke to her and held her as they danced. No wonder good girls went astray, she thought. She touched hands with many people over the years and no one had created that kind of electric response in her. Sparks flew. She wondered if he felt it too. Surely, it couldn't happen to only her.

William came to call on her and asked her mother's permission to court her. Sarah agreed. Her solicitor had assured her, "William Dean Davis is a nice young man and would make a suitable husband. He comes from good stock; however, they're not wealthy just nicely situated. His mother had a small inheritance and his father had a small well-run farm with a good bit of timber land. His family is well thought of in the community."

At first, he was the perfect gentleman. He listened to her thoughts and plans. Telling her all the places he wanted to go, and the goals he wanted to achieve. It was fun and lively to be with him and walk around the grounds and picnic under the trees. They rode out on horses. He seemed fascinated with the land, ponds and streams. They talked about the wildlife they saw and listened to the birds. Eva shared the special places of her beloved Amber

Manor with him.

Too soon, he tried to kiss her. She told him, "No sir, I'll not have any of that! We haven't known each other long enough for that kind of goings on."

"How long do I have to wait? I don't want to wait one minute longer than is necessary."

"If that's all you're about then leave me alone. You need not return if you can't control yourself. If my father were alive, he would have you flogged and never allow you on the place again."

"Eva don't be that way. I'm sorry. I didn't mean to offend you. Some girls like to be kissed." He wheedled himself back into her good graces. It was her first mistake. He showed his character and she let him get away with it. Why must he be so handsome and almost the only one she liked, who had come as a caller after the ball? A girl gets a little scared that the world will pass her by when she has her Coming Out Ball, and only a few eligible bachelors come to call.

Several others had asked to come courting. One was a contemporary of my father's. Mother read his note and stamped her feet. "How dare that old goat ask to court you? Your father never liked him anyway. And I would rather be dead than see you wed to the likes of Morris Fleming!"

"Thank you, Mother." She tossed her head. "He always smells of an awful cigar."

Peter Sullivan, a wealthy, young gentleman and a bit of a snob, wanted to marry, but was not sure she had the highly developed social graces he looked for in the woman who would share his life. Perhaps he could train her and if she worked out, they could possibly marry.

Her mother was in the room when he spouted his declaration to her. Sarah had jumped to her feet and told the servant coming into the room with tea for us, "Leave it and go." The girl scurried out.

Mother turned on Mr. Sullivan. "I can't believe you would come here to an innocent young girl who just came out, looking for your next mistress! Train her indeed. How dare you? Get out of my house. If you tell a soul you even made such an indecent proposition to my daughter, I'll surely blacken your name and tell all I have ever heard about you. OUT!"

Her mother looked stricken and Eva thought she might have a heart attack. She sank down into a burgundy chair and cried into her handkerchief. Eva sat at her feet like a small child trying to comfort her.

The experience was why she contacted the solicitor when the note from William and other young men arrived. They both thought it was prudent to check them out. Solicitors must not know much about a person with a murderous heart.

It was even colder now. William's horse should have arrived back at the stable and the hands should be out looking for them by now. She could ride back and leave William, she shuddered. She must act in a proper manner. Especially since she would never tell what he tried to do, or that the ghost of her long dead Grandmother saved her.

Her thoughts jumped all over the place. She prayed. *Lord send help quickly please.*

She thought back "*William you're acting silly.*

We cannot marry for at least a year. It would scandalize me if we hurriedly had a wedding. Do men never consider the woman's purity? You're constantly shocking me with your rush to get married. It's not proper. The courtship is the time to get to know about each other and if there is enough love and mutual bond to last a lifetime."

"It has been over six months. My desire for you is so great, we must marry soon, or I'll go mad. Women have no idea how much power they have over a man's body. I've been patient. You act like a child. You still won't let me kiss you and show you what a real woman wants from a man. I should find someone else. You probably want to be a spinster, alone all your life. No one else will want to marry you. You're blushing and look like a scared rabbit. If you're going to cry, I'm leaving. If you won't marry me next month, I may not come back."

Would she be an old maid, was he right, that no one would want to be her husband? Did she want him to stay or leave? Mother had spent so much to bring her out. What if no partner wanted her? She might feel crushed. Was he being mean, as she thought or was it her immaturity that made her think that way? If she rushed into marriage, she would lose honor and respect from her friends and community. If she insisted they wait, she might lose William.

"You'll have to do what you think best, William. I must go inside now. Good-bye." She turned and enjoyed the flounce of the lavender dress as she swished past him and headed for the door. He reached out and grabbed her arm roughly. "Eva, don't ever walk away from me. I'm leaving but you had better learn to mind your manners."

She watched as he strode down to the stable to get his horse. Her arm was sore for a week where he had squeezed it. He didn't return for two weeks and she was sure she had lost him. Her only chance at happiness was gone.

When he came back, Eva found her mother and William in the parlor. It was evident he didn't like the conversation they had been having when she walked into the room. She greeted them both and sat in her favorite chair, the big green one with the lace doilies on the arms. She put her feet on the footstool and waited for them to continue the talk.

Mother said, "William has been telling me of his urgent need to wed you before the agreed upon wedding date as previously set. I have refused permission for any such event. We are decent God-fearing people, and I'll not condone a breech such as this outrageous idea. Convention has a place and keeps society on track. Either you will submit to our rules or the wedding is off, permanently. Perhaps you have gambling debts that would make Eva's money look very appealing. If you need it sooner than the date set for the wedding. Is that the problem Mr. Davis?"

We watched his face turn red.

"No, Madam. Money is not involved in this discussion."

Sarah gave a dismissive wave of her hand. "Then go now and let me know what you decide."

William stood and bowed to her. "I'll decide. Eva, come with me."

"I have business to discuss with Eva; she will stay right where she is now."

Eva smiled at William. "Good-bye, see you soon."

He steamed out of the house.

A month later he returned, very contrite. The marriage took place as planned with all their friends and family in attendance. The church was full, and it was ablaze with candles, and the flowers from their home were in abundance. Her wedding gown was perfect, made by the same seamstress who made her ball gowns. She couldn't believe her dressmaker could outdo the other gowns, but she did. She wore her grandmother's amber necklace as her something old. Katherine gave her a white satin garter for something new. Mother loaned her a fancy lace handkerchief for something borrowed and Martha the cook gave her a blue satin ribbon for something blue, it was tied to her white and yellow rose bouquet. Eva was happy standing at the altar with her tall handsome dark-haired prince.

Who knew he would turn into a murderer? I want to scream again. William tried to kill me. Murder me. Pushed me with great force and with a crazed look in his eyes.

Chapter 4

She hoped help would arrive soon. Eva wanted to go home. She was confused and shattered; her thoughts ran wild. Her life with William took over her mind.

"Eva, you need to have your proper friends over for cards or tea or even small dinner parties. Cultivate the upper class. Invite your higher, well thought of, more appropriate friends to our home. You know the people of the Town Society, bring them here." William harped on those ideas often.

She still let him believe her friends in the upper-class society would be glad to have them attend their parties even though she didn't feel she could take him to their parties or invite them to one at Amber Manor. It was easier to make excuses why they couldn't attend those events and keep up polite correspondence as if all were well with her. Mother still attended parties and stayed with her friends, but they told William that she was visiting and not that there was a big supper or party involved. She knew she would have to tell him he wasn't welcome at some time, but she wasn't ready to do it yet.

From the start of their union, William spoke badly of Katherine. He couldn't understand Eva's friendship with the housekeeper. It was fine for two old maids to bond together in their loneliness and mutual disdain of men, or children who knew no better. He thought they spent too much time together reading, sewing, and talking. "What can a housekeeper have in common with the Lady of the house? Eva, are you just a low gossip? That attitude must come from your mother, she also holds that girl in too high regard." Or he would out and out say, "Katherine is incompetent. You must dismiss her immediately. She was insubordinate to me. She sulks around the house and undermines my authority every chance she gets."

Eva asked, "How has she done that?"

"You always do that. You're against me too; don't believe what your own husband says, over a mere servant. Get her out of the house. It riles me up to look at her."

William started to go to the city and stay away for two or three days at a time. When she inquired what he did when he was away from home, he promptly told her, "It's not any of your business, all you need to be concerned about is taking care of my needs when I'm home."

William began to invite his city friends to their home for weekend parties. They often lasted an entire week. If she refused to associate with the elite and have parties for them, he would bring his friends home. None of the women had anything to say that made sense to Eva.

All the money spent for these entertainments began to add up. "How can we keep this up, if he continues to be so lavish? Worthless, scoundrel, no good and shady are words, my father would have used for him." Eva told Katherine.

Since William ran with the likes of those fellows, was it his true nature? She had just seen his true nature, MURDERER! He tried to kill her by pushing her off a horse running as fast as it could go. Her neck would have been broken instead of his, and he would have claimed it was an accident. As her husband, he would have inherited everything. The land and house left to her by her grandparents, Amber Manor, and the farms and money. That must be why he did it. Surely, she hadn't been that bad of a wife.

Could I have done anything that would have changed what happened? she asked herself.

She didn't believe William would have married Pearl Garver. He would have looked for someone better favored with stature in the community. Pearl wouldn't have fared well. With her money and lands he would have become a more desirable husband for a woman of higher rank than Pearl. A woman who also had wealth, and perhaps a higher title than Eva's.

I wonder how many women he would have married and killed. Thank God, his life has ended. I'll never tell about Grandmother saving me with the Amulet of Safety. Or that her ghost scared the horse and caused William's death, she told herself again.

Their marriage hadn't worked from the start. The wonderful person she thought she had exchanged vows with vanished. Out came the evil inside him. He was cruel, mean, petty, jealous and manipulative.

When she confronted him about Pearl Garver he hit her across the face and pushed her into an overstuffed chair. He leaned over her and pinned her arms down. He said, "All men have mistresses. It's expected of us."

"Not by the new wife, that's for sure!" She shouted back at him and received another hard slap.

"You're such a prude that a man would prefer a mistress to you. No wonder no one else will ever want you. You make me sick." He walked out of the room slamming the heavy door. William didn't return for over a month.

Life with him gone was more tolerable. He came back and acted as though nothing happened. He wanted us to ride every day as usual. To kill me must have been his plan all along. What really made her mad is that she allowed him to deceive her. Did she want to believe him so much that she would let herself be blinded to his true feelings?

She grew weary and prayed the men from Amber Manor would find them soon. They would take care of William's body and take her home. She was sick and weak. He had tried to kill her. It seemed such a long time since she'd seen Grandmother's ghost. She was cold. Was it just her or had the whole world turned cold and dreary?

Maybe she died and was all alone. Must she sit there forever as punishment? Did she do something wrong that she didn't even remember? Did God banish her?

A Bible verse came into her mind. *"I am with you always, even unto the ends of the earth."*

Maybe the end had come, left her, and she wasn't taken with Jesus. Old Preacher McHenry always shouted about fire and brimstone. *"Be prepared. Get right with God, right this minute!"* he would say.

"God, please make me right with you, I pray. Please hear me and guide me through whatever comes from this death. He tried to kill me. Thank You, for sending Grandmother. I would like to talk to her. Why did she go first to Katherine, when we found the Amulet? Help me! God, I know, you already did by keeping me on my horse. Thank You for your love. Amen."

Eva closed her eyes and waited. There was nothing to do right then but wait for the men to arrive.

Maybe she could pull her skirts up closer to her and get warmer. As she adjusted them, she touched the amulet in her pocket. Her hand instantly warmed. She would keep holding it to stave off the chill. It got warmer and she could feel calmness wash over her body.

After a time, she saw the men coming to help her. It would be some time before they reached her. It seemed odd to see them from so far away, a group of men heading toward her. She wondered how long until she could recognize them. Knowing they were on their way gave her great comfort. Waiting patiently was hard. She wanted them to hurry, make their horses run faster.

Joseph Moore, the land manager, led the men in the search. He spotted her and raced harder to reach them. All came with purpose and haste. The hardy men rode tall in their saddles being almost one with their mounts. Both men and horses were well trained. Most of the horses were bred and raised on the Manor and were some of the best stock in the world.

Joseph took in the whole scene before him. He jumped off his horse in front of her and asked, "Miss Eva, are you alright? Are you injured?"

She shook her head. "No."

"What happened? We started the search as soon as Mr. William's horse came running into the stable area all lathered up and spooked so bad, we thought he had seen a ghost. I sent parties out in all directions so we could find you faster. I'm glad our group found you."

She started to speak. A horrible screech was all that came out. *I almost yelled out "That, horrible man tried to kill me!" But a presence stopped my words.*

Chapter 5

*J*oseph told the men to untie their horse blankets and he took off his own. He wrapped it around her and told the men she must be in shock. He gave orders for Adam, James, and Charlie to wrap William and put him on a horse and follow behind. Joseph mounted and two of the men lifted her up in front of him.

Just then, she saw what they were doing and screamed out, "NO! DON'T PUT HIM ON MY HORSE!"

Charlie almost fell as he held the dead man, ready to heft him over her horse Candy's saddle. Joseph said, "Alright Miss Eva, we will put him on another horse. Can someone else ride your horse back home?"

She nodded. "Yes."

The command obeyed the men scrambled to use

another horse. The long ride back was difficult. She was exhausted. Joseph was having no problem holding her wrapped almost like a mummy. The blanket was tight with not much give to it, so she was unable to bend in places you need to bend to sit on a horse. The wool blankets were heavy, thick, and a bit scratchy. She was too warm. Eva was grateful Joseph rescued her.

She needed to stop thinking about the recent events so she could calm down. Eva slumped forward a little and thought of the spring flowers she loved so much each year. Amber Manor Gardens were the talk of people all over the country. Unannounced, a group of foreign travelers came to visit several years ago. They had met a friend of her father's, Albert Abernathy, and he had told them her father would be delighted to provide them hospitality and show them his beautiful grounds. Father was thrilled that his friend had honored him in such a way.

The cook made more food, and rooms were made up and the twelve of them stayed at the Manor two weeks. Her father loved entertaining. Joy filled the house it was a good time for all.

She couldn't stay slumped as she was, it was painful. As she moved upright, Joseph pulled her against his shoulder. It was a comfort and nice.

When they arrived home, she would take a bath and sleep.

She had duties to perform. A funeral was such a detestable business. The undertaker needed to be notified, arrangements made, and food prepared. It would take a ton of food. Everyone in the country attended a funeral. Many brought food and flowers with them. All the people who worked and lived on the Manor's land and several farms around about would arrive, plus, all their social acquaintances, and friends and family. On funeral days all class distinctions were not observed, thank goodness.

Eva would be pitied and petted and most surely on display. Had she cried much, been seared to the heart from the loss of her loved one? Was she relieved? This was a concern if there had been a long illness. If that was the case, she would be told, by people, *"He is in a better place (even if he was a known scoundrel),"and "it is a blessing, no more pain for him"* She wanted to cry from the fact that the ordeal was in front of her. Crying for herself might ease the people around her and maybe be good for her since she couldn't yell out, *"William had murder in his heart! He held no love for me. I sure can't cry anymore tears for him."*

It seemed to take forever to get home, more time than it took to go somewhere. It was the same distance. Maybe the excitement of going keeps your spirits up so the time quickly passes. When the journey ends people were tired from the exertion of the day. Mother had told them *"Kids always ask, are we there yet, coming and going?"* Maybe it seemed more tiring on the way home because the excitement was gone.

Joseph said in her ear, "You can see the house through the trees. I'll have you home and warm soon. Doctor Webb will probably be there waiting. We sent for him as soon as we started the search. I sent men to let the other search groups know we found you so all the hands should be arriving too. Before we get back, I wanted to tell you how sorry I am you saw such a sight, and endured Williams accident. You were brave to wait there for us to find you. It was the right thing to do. After such a trauma, you might have gotten lost. I saw you bristle, just then. I know you're a good rider and know the grounds well, but I think you're in a state of shock. In circumstances such as this accident that's to be expected. If there is ever anything any of us can do to help you just ask."

"Thank you."

They were silent the rest of the way home.

She had an inquisition coming. She would have to face everything on her own. As weak and helpless as she felt, she needed to be strong and get through all the questions and remember what she said. No sympathetic moves on her part. No yelling, screaming, and telling people off when they told her what a good man her husband was for her. No indication that there was ever anything but bliss and joy in their union. She could do all things through Christ who strengthened her.

Now she saw why the Sunday school teacher made her learn those verses so they would come to her in times of need. She thought, *"God, send your strength to guard my tongue."* She needed to be ready, whether she was or not.

As they neared her home she began to cry. It was such a welcome and beautiful sight, the gray stones with the sunshine on them made the amber color that created its famous name, Amber Manor. She was thankful to be alive to see it.

Katherine, mother, and the doctor ran down the steps toward her.

Katherine reached her first. "Oh, thank God you're safe," she said, then she spotted the horse carrying William's body. "Oh," she said.

Eva looked her in the eye and said, "We'll talk later."

She knew her so well, Katherine got the message that she would tell her the real story when they were alone. She had always been a friend to lean on during the hard times. At that moment, Eva was glad to have that knowledge. She was blessed not to be alone.

A couple of the men lifted her from Joseph's lap. He got off the horse and picked her up and asked mother where her room was located. He carried her up the stairs and put her gently down on the bed.

He unwrapped his blanket and folded it, pulled the comforter from the foot of the bed and covered her. He straightened up taking his hat off and bowed. "Miss Eva, the doctor will see to you now. I'll leave you in his good hands." With that, he left the room.

Eva listened to his footfalls on the wood floors.

She remembered her newly dead husband would be laid out in the parlor downstairs. She had strong feelings for William when she first met him; look where that got her. She ended up with a man who tried to kill her! Would she ever forget the words "murderer" and "kill me?"

She loved to read mysteries with Katherine. Before she married and when her husband was away, they would read for hours in the big wing backed chairs with their feet on the ottoman. After reading they discussed their books in the comfort of the cozy library. Would she enjoy it again? It was quite another matter to be on the inside of a crime, nearly a dead victim, with a broken neck. She braced herself as she heard a group come up the stairs.

The doctor asked first. "What happened? That boy downstairs looked positively scared to death. Are you injured? Did you fall too?"

She opened her eyes. "We were racing, his horse got spooked and shied, when he pulled the reins, the horse reared up on his hind legs. William was tossed into the tree. He was dead."

"Do you know what spooked the horse?" he asked.

"Who knows about such things?"

Mother wrung her hands. "Darling, are you hurt?"

Eva knew her mother didn't get upset easily. "No, Mother. It was William who ended up with a broken neck." That was the truth. She hadn't been the one to die as he planned.

Katherine looked on. She had caught the underlying words not spoken.

The doctor shooed everyone from the room and said, "Out, I must tend to the patient."

Once they were gone, he asked. "Are you with child?"

"Not that I know of." *Oh, dear God, please don't let that have happened. I'm being strong but that's beyond me.*

After he examined her, he pronounced, "You're

still in shock and need to sleep. I'll give the housekeeper some laudanum and instruct her how to give it to you. It will be hard to attend all the activities associated with a funeral, but you can do it. I'm sorry for your loss, Miss Eva."

She grabbed his hand and asked, "Can I just sleep through the event? Skip the whole thing. Can you say I'm under doctor's care and can't be disturbed? Please doctor. I don't think I can stand all those gossipy women. I know most mean well, but some are mean and unkind."

"Don't act like a silly little girl. I know this is difficult. People are what they are, and we can't change them. But we must live among them and it helps to go to a funeral and say our good-byes to loved ones. When the funeral is over, you'll feel you have done all that was possible for your husband and can move on with life.

"If I let you do as you want, you might continue to hide from the world. That would be tragic. You're young and vital. I'm not saying the next lightly. You will find another love to make you happy. Time is a healer of the heart. Give yourself time. Society has rules of conduct that can be of great benefit if we abide by them. Wear your black for a season. Make and receive the polite calls on friends and family as dictated. Take the medicine and sleep for a while. Eat good nourishing food.

"I have been invited to supper. You have a special cook. Join the others as soon as you feel like it tomorrow. I have ordered you food before the medicine. I'll check on you before I go."

He had to turn his hand to release himself from

her grip. Doctor Webb had delivered her into this world. His kindness and wisdom were well established. She knew he was right but didn't want to let him go. His old face crinkled into a slight smile as he freed his hand.

"It doesn't seem like it now, but life will get better again. I know from experience. The beautiful glow will come to your face one day. This sadness will fade. You may always love William, but your heart will open as a rose petal to welcome other loved ones inside your heart. Oh, here is our girl with your supper. I know girls don't like to eat when they're so downtrodden, but you must keep up your strength. Eat, I'll be back." He smiled and nodded at Katherine as he walked out the door and went down the stairs.

Katherine came into the room and sat the food tray on the bedside table. She helped Eva bring her feet around to sit on the bedside. She was happy Katherine had brought two dinners and coffee to eat with her.

It was like old times, friends having dinner as they had done all their lives before she married.

"Eva, your mother will be up before long. I think she aged ten years while we waited to hear what happened to you. We knew it was awful when told how badly spooked Williams horse was and how long it took the hands to calm him down. We did take heart, that it was his horse that had returned in a frenzied state, not yours. Do you want to tell me what happened?"

Katherine sat on the bed beside Eva and gave her a big hug then went to her chair and poured the coffee. A hot cup of coffee tasted better than ever before. They ate a little.

"Eva, do you think William took the amulet? Your grandmother told us, it was stolen so harm could be done to you. Luckily no one checked to see if it was still in the can of old unused nails. Please tell me what happened to you?"

"He must have taken it. William had been extra nice since he came back this time and tried to please me. We have been going on our daily rides with a picnic Martha fixed us. After enjoying it we walked the horses then raced back. Today we stopped by the stream at a favorite place of ours. He reached out and took my hand, then told me he wanted us to go to Italy for a month or so. Telling me about the vineyards we would see, delightful foods, like ravioli, spaghetti, lasagna all made with wonderful cheeses and served with wine. He said we could take bicycle trips to close areas of interest and roam around the plazas. It was a fabulous picture of our trip he had planned. The day was perfect. I thought all problems worked out and life was good. I was so wrong.

He had spun a web of lies and I believed them all. We enjoyed the day, talked and laughed so much my sides ached." Eva paused and thought about what she had just said.

Katherine poured more coffee and they both drank deeply. Her hazel eyes shimmered. She was sharing her friend's pain. Eva noticed clearly the blue of her dress complimented them well. It must have been the shade of blue that brought out their beauty. She thought it funny to think of such trivial things now, such as the color of her friend's, eyes and dress, at a time like this. But her mind had bounced around all afternoon. Maybe it was a way for people to cope with tragedy, by noticing the common things, they normally wouldn't think about.

"William kissed me long and well, and then said, 'We better hurry home for more of this. I'll get there first today.' He mounted his horse and started. The race was on. We were running full out when I caught up to him and pulled ahead. He came from behind and moved his horse too close beside me. He reached across and pushed me as hard as he could, almost waist level, unseating me. I was shocked, and falling off my horse. I couldn't do anything about it. Giant hands went around my waist and righted me in my saddle, and I sat solid once again. I saw Grandmother's ghost in front of us. I turned my horse away from her.

"William's horse must have seen Grandmother's ghost in his way. William screamed as his horse reared and tossed him off. He hit the tree they were passing with a loud thud. Grandmother was gone, I could see so was William. I walked my horse around a few minutes, then leaned down on Candy's neck and talked quietly, soothing until she calmed. I sat on my horse looking at the handsome man who was no more. His face wore a horrified mask. I tied Candy to a small tree branch and sat down to wait for the men from the farm to come for me, and cried a little for being so stupid. I was glad it was over."

Katherine cried silently, as shocked by the story,

as Eva was by the telling of it. We finished the food and apple pie with a cheese slice on top. Eva was hungry.

"I have been wondering why Grandmother's ghost spoke to you first when we found the amulet? She didn't talk to me after William died. I thought she should have said something at least. I was alone a long time."

Katherine wiped her tears with her napkin. "I don't know. I was so upset about the lost necklace. Maybe that opened a path for her to communicate with me. Maybe she thought you should be with me when we found it. She might have thought you would tell William. It's possible that she knew he hid it. You took a bit of persuading to get you to wear it and not tell anyone."

"I was thankful to have it this afternoon. I was falling to the ground. It was a miracle. I think an angel caught me and lifted me and put me back on Candy today. If Grandmother hadn't helped us find the Amulet of Safety, I would be the one in the parlor with a broken neck. When I waited with the body of my husband, I screamed, "'Murderer!'" over and over for such a long, long time. He tried to kill me! I couldn't get past that idea. The man who had taken vows with me, tried to murder me."

"Maybe your grandmother will be able to talk to you, and help you understand. Or maybe there is no understanding on this side of heaven. Perhaps there is no answer to why or why me? Why must I endure this situation? You thought an angel helped you back into the saddle today so that means God will help you through everything. There is a reason you're alive tonight. I think I hear your mother on the stairs. I'll let you talk to her then bring in the medicine the doctor left for you to sleep. I love you, friend. I'll help any way I can."

Katherine left, as Mother stepped into her room.

"Mother, did Doctor Webb enjoy his meal? He sure likes Martha's cooking."

"Dear, you don't have to be brave for me. But yes, he enjoyed it and demanded to kiss the cook. She let him." Sarah said.

"While she was in the dining room he said, 'I once tried to lure Martha away from you. She didn't want anything but true love. I told her, I truly loved her cooking.' Martha and all gathered laughed. It helped lighten the mood. He said you're fine, just spooked like Williams horse and when you were calmed you would continue as good as new. He told us you would look good in black and about his lecture on holding to proprieties. He will be up to see about you in a little while. Has Katherine brought the medicine yet?" she asked.

"No, Mother she will give it to me after my visit with you. She is truly my friend. I'm sorry you had to be worried like that all afternoon while the men looked for us. I was glad to see you come down the stairs when I got here. Thank you for being my mother, I love you."

"Eva, I love you too. Families don't say that enough. Daily we go about and think we are invincible. Then an accident happens, and life becomes most precious. From now on we should give our blessings and good wishes often, is that alright with you? My mother used to say, give me my flowers while I'm here to enjoy them not after I'm gone."

"Word of William's death has already gone abroad. We must plan the funeral. Do you think you can help with that tomorrow?" her mother asked.

"It will probably be afternoon. I'll sleep late if the medicine works. I hope it does, my mind is unsettled. I want to sleep," Eva said.

Mother got up from the chair, came over to the bed, kissed me, and gave me a big hug. "I never wanted to interfere in your marriage, but perhaps this is for the best. God knows how to help us even when we don't know which way to go. Good night, my lovely girl."

"Good night, Mother. I love you." She seemed relieved her daughter was unharmed. Eva would never be fine, but mother didn't know that.

Doctor Webb knocked on the door. He looked her over. "I predict you should be out of bed in the morning as soon as the laudanum wears off. Your mother is putting me up for the night, so I'll see you tomorrow when you awaken."

"I heard you tried to run off with Martha," Eva said.

He sighed, "She thought I was kidding. I always kidded around her because I was nervous. She wanted true love and I foolishly said, 'I truly love your cooking.' She laughed and has made it a joke all these years. Good night sweet girl."

Katherine entered with the little vial of sleep. She was very careful about the amount she administered. Eva noticed she took the bottle back with her after wishing her friend goodnight.

Sleep came over her like a heavy blanket. Her mind got sluggish and her eyelids heavy. This was not a nice restful sleep but an overwhelming of the senses. Her last thought was, would she ever be able to come out of this in the morning?

She awoke about noon and needed help to get out of the bed. She was groggy like she imagined someone would feel from drinking for days on end. She reached for the bell pull, closed her eyes and waited. Katherine arrived with hot coffee, eggs scrambled, crispy bacon, and biscuits with orange marmalade. She set it on the table and helped Eva sit on the bedside. The lavender walls and furnishings looked way too bright and made her eyes ache. She said, "I always loved this room but now it looks garish. It's odd I wasn't hurt and yet now I ache all over and my head, eyes, ears and teeth hurt. Like each of them pounded my aching head. I never want any more of that medicine."

Katherine smiled. "Doctor Webb said you would feel that way. But that was the only way he knew to get the sleep you needed without any nightmares of yesterday's events. He also said you must eat hardy as you have many decisions to make and work to do." Katherine sat opposite of Eva and watched her eat breakfast and had a cup of coffee with her. Her housekeeper caught her up on the household events. The laundress's daughter was with child again. Martha had a great niece getting married. Their usual banter about the stable hands and farm boys was discussed. They talked about the livestock and the gardens and everyday life on Amber Manor.

Eva needed help to get dressed and go down the

stairs. Thank God for Katherine. She led her into the morning room where Mother liked to spend her leisure time. Sarah sat at the desk and wrote notes to the people whom she needed to invite to attend the funeral. As they entered, she looked up and so did Doctor Webb.

Greetings exchanged, Katherine helped her to the deep brown leather chair. She then left the room to prepare the afternoon tea.

Doctor Webb said, "By teatime the rest of the laudanum should have worn off and you can walk and move on your own. The food you just ate, and the afternoon tea will also help the headache go away. If you feel like sleeping, go ahead and do so. Your mother and I have been working on the funeral arrangements. Would you like the warm shawl there pulled up over your shoulders?"

"No thank you. I'm warm enough right now. If I need it later, I'll ask. I do feel a little drowsy but I'm hoping to come out of that."

Mother asked, "Eva is there anything special you want done for the funeral? I have already sent a dispatch to William's parents. The answer back was that they would arrive early Saturday morning and return home the same day. They're taking it hard, too. They want to bury him in the family plot at their home."

She burst out with, "Thank God for that. I don't want him in our..." the rest of the words faded away when she realized what she'd said. Both the other people in the room stared at her dumbfounded. Because of her outburst, she tried to save the blunder. "It would be so hard having him right here.

Doctor you said I would heal from this dramatic turn of events but if he is here, I think it would be so much more difficult to continue with life and to look forward. The funeral here will make it indelible that he is forever gone, like you told me last night.

"Maybe he will be a comfort to his mother there." She figured she had better stop talking before she got deeper into trouble. Eva sat wringing her handkerchief in distress. Kind eyes met hers when she looked up at them a minute or two later.

Sarah said, "That will be best for the parents, I'm sure. You're being gracious allowing them to take their boy home as they have requested. As his wife, you could have refused. I'm proud of you for allowing them this kindness."

Sarah pointed out the stacks of notes she had already written to their friends in the Ton and others. "Eva you will need to rejoin your old acquaintances and attend their parties and house visits when proper time has elapsed for mourning. When I have attended without you, they all tell me how much they miss you. And I have heard there is speculation on your excuses for being out of their company. Many will arrive for the funeral out of curiosity not friendship, to collect gossip to pass to the ones who don't get here. You must pretend you don't see or hear anything derogatory. It will be an ordeal. I wish I could protect you from them but I'm sure you will handle it with grace and patience."

"Mother, I never told you, but William wasn't welcome at some of the events because of his actions at our wedding and that big ball we attended in London. After I was told about it, I didn't tell him we were invited and made excuses and always ask you to go and make my apologies. I wasn't sure whose feelings he hurt. I wasn't told the details, so I decided I would stay away from all the activities and maybe after time passed, we could venture into their midst again. He was always mad that I didn't invite our friends of the Ton to Amber Manor and couldn't figure out why you were invited but we weren't. I felt it was better not to let him know he had offended several of them. He thought I was prudish and didn't want him around other women because I was jealous. I think I did the prudent thing by letting him believe what he would. After the proper amount of time I can ease back into society. It will be nice to belong again."

Eva would be happy to restart her society rounds again and have people visit her at Amber Manor. It would be like before she married William. Life would go on without him.

Sarah nodded and smiled at her daughter. "Now we must get the arrangements for the funeral made. Is there a special song he liked, or you prefer?"

"Thank you, Mother. William liked the dirge the Pastor had the organist play when he was going to bring us a real hellfire and damnation sermon. I like the Twenty-Third Psalm. Will Preacher McHenry do the officiating?" She had been to his funerals before and he would preach a good one, but it might be awful sitting that long.

Sarah said. "He volunteered, expecting to be paid, however. We have had great response without special invitation. People will descend on us from all directions. Cook has sent out the clarion call for any in reach of us to help with the food. Thank God we have a full farm, so the food is available. I think I saw a dozen pies and several cakes as I came through the kitchen. I picked out your favorite cake for our tea this afternoon."

Sarah was past ready for coffee. "Doctor, Eva would you like some coffee now?"

They agreed, and she rang the bell for a servant. They worked on the plans, drank their coffee and worked some more, until it was teatime at last. Eva was hungry and had regained strength. Her favorite cake was butter pecan with rum sauce liberally poured over the top.

Several finger sandwiches were offered. She always chose a couple of the watercress and a couple of the cucumber. Martha wouldn't tell them what her secret sauce ingredient was that she added to them. Several kinds of cookies and a few candies were always served too. And the best part was the tea, she thought it must be the best in the world. She had visited many places that served disastrous tea. With theirs she never added anything to it. Other places she tasted then added as needed. It was an art to make tea just right.

The thought struck her. *When we grieved, we talked about and did so many other things not associated with it. Then it hits you in the face again and you're in woe. It seemed our minds cycle back and forth with regular everyday need to do thoughts and sorrow.* They talked and worked on until supper time. Tomorrow would be another busy day. Eva slept well with no medicine side effects.

Chapter 6

aturday, the household was up bustling about at six a.m. as usual. William's parents arrived at seven-thirty. Sarah planned to put them up in a nice room she had the maids prepare for them. They were such nice people. How could they have produced a monster? This and the wedding were Eva's only meetings with them.

They had traveled to Amber Manor for the wedding and arrived two days before the event. Mother and Eva had been impressed with them and thought William would be a good match because of his parents, pleasant dinner conversation and knowledge. Sarah was busy with the preparations for the wedding but when she found out that they were interested in plants she had the gardener take them through the gardens and gave them cuttings of several flowers and vegetable plants they were interested in growing.

Before going to their room today, they met with Eva in the sitting room. Elmer Davis had aged well, an older version of William. He stood by the fireplace. His wife, Sally, a petite dark-haired woman sat in a chair next to him. She looked drawn as she twisted her handkerchief. Her eyes gave away her precious tears.

"Well girl, what happened?" Elmer said gently.

"William and I took our daily ride. We took a picnic. The day was beautiful, and we stopped several places. We watched the ducks on the pond and saw geese fly by. We ate by the pond and saw a fox in the woods on our way back. We held hands and were enjoying all life had to offer. William mounted his horse and we started our regular race toward home. He caught up to me and his horse spooked. He yelled as he fell. The horse reared and threw him against a tree. He died instantly. He didn't suffer," she said.

"What spooked his horse?" his father asked.

"My horse was fine, so I don't see how one horse could get spooked and the other not. One moment we were racing and the next his horse reared and tossed William. The horse ran off, I had a time getting mine to calm down. I went and sat by William until the riders from the estate arrived and found us. It was both horrible and a great shock." Eva said.

"Yes girl, I can imagine. You did right by sitting with him no matter how awful it was to stay there. People think they're going to get help and get themselves lost instead. You are a fine horsewoman and you knew the rider-less horse would return to the stable and a search party would come to look for you. We are sorry you had to endure this hardship. I'm sure your mother told you we would like to take William home with us for burial. I know as his wife you probably want him here with you. Sally would really appreciate your letting us do this, me too."

Eva said, "I have discussed it with my mother, and she encouraged me to let you take him. Since you have had him so much longer, I will allow it. Have you brought a cart to transport him or would you like us to provide one? I'm sorry for your loss."

"We hold you in high esteem daughter-in-law. We came prepared with a wagon, believing you to be a tenderhearted and considerate young woman. What I have to say now is for your future clear mind. I don't know if we will see you after today, so we wanted to say it now." He looked at his wife and she nodded at him and then Eva and gave a little smile. "You're a beautiful young girl. You're hurt now with this loss. But you must look toward the future when another man will want to marry you. We wanted you to know when that time comes to you that you have our blessing. We would never want you to be pining away your life. May you have many children; and grow to be an old woman, God Bless you," William's father said.

"Thank you for your graciousness. I can't see that happening. But that you hold these kind thoughts for me will be cherished forever." Real tears fell from Eva's eyes.

Katherine entered and announced. "Cook has

your breakfast ready. Please follow me to the dining room. When you're finished eating, I'll show you to the room Mrs. Sarah had prepared for you."

They all stood; hugged each other and they left. She sat down and cried, really cried. "Why was William so different from them? How does a bad, evil person come from good parents?" She hoped they never heard how mean he was in his life. "God, please shield these nice people from the knowledge of his cruelty and dishonor. May they never know he was cheating on me and most especially that William tried to kill me," she prayed.

Mother found her asleep in the chair with tears on her cheeks. She gently leaned over and shook her shoulder and said, "Eva it's time to get ready for the funeral."

When she got up, Mother gave her a good hug and a big smile and said, "You and all of us can do this. Tomorrow this part will be over, and we can move forward. I really like William's parents. They thanked me for encouraging you to let them bury William at their home. That made them as happy as they can be under the circumstances. I'm proud of you my daughter. We'd better hurry and put on those good black dresses." They went upstairs arm and arm to do just that.

Chairs were set up on the back lawn where ample trees shaded them. All the chairs were full, and people were sitting on blankets all over behind the chairs. Clothes ran from peasant finery to high society best. Eva sat in a black taffeta dress that had been her standard funeral garb for several years. Now she had to be totally outfitted in a complete black wardrobe. The dressmaker who made her ball gown and wedding dress had contacted mother as soon as she got word of William's demise. She had been engaged, soon the whole widows' weeds collection would be in her closet and she would be expected to be seen in nothing else for an entire year as dictated by society.

The doctor told her how nice she looked in black. He seems to be enjoying his indefinite visit. When he was called to Amber Manor for the emergency, he left word where he was going and since then let his office girl know of his extended stay.

Too many flowers gave off a cloying scent. Maybe that was just her opinion but everyone else seemed in awe over their beauty. The handmade wooden coffin was beautiful with a real nice fine-looking finish. She wondered who made it. They sure did lovely woodworking. A scroll work design went around the front and sides. She guessed it went all around but that was all she could see.

Old Preacher McHenry walked to the front of the casket, thanked everyone for their attendance, and started. "First of all, I want to tell all the family and friends gathered here today, I'm sorry for your loss. This fine young specimen of a man was too young to die. But he did. Each of you are too young to die. But like William here, we never know when it will be our time. So, you must always be ready to step out of this life and into eternity. Each of us will stand before Almighty God."

Eva didn't think she heard another word. The proceedings went on for what seemed like hours.

She couldn't think of William. She must shut her mind to him. The people present didn't know he tried to murder her. She must think of something else or she would start to shout. If she ever started to scream, she might not be able to stop.

Her grandmother once told a story of an old preacher who shot himself. Everyone in the country thought his wife killed him. They had the funeral, and everyone went to see if she would break down and admit she did it.

The day was as hot as Hades. The flowers were so many they had to put some in the basement. As the day got hotter the many flowers inside and the scent from the ones downstairs had people about to faint. It was overwhelming. Six preachers insisted they speak since he was their minister-friend. The service went on and on and on. Even with a closed casket, it took over two hours to go through the viewing line and shake all the hands. They had a big potluck dinner on the grounds, which took a couple more hours.

When grandmother and her mother got home, they decided, "If the wife did kill him, she sure got enough punishment today for a lifetime." Going through the funeral and all the advice, questions and inquisition was enough punishment for her.

William's funeral was over. Many friends attended and it was good to see them, and she was glad to see them leave. The day had been long and trying. She had to get to bed. Eva slept well considering her husband was dead and on his way with his parents. What a relief.

She got up early, had breakfast and went to

church. They went back to their regular Sunday routine. People don't value schedules as much as they should, and don't notice it; some think it dull and boring. But the structure helped people when otherwise they would lose their way. It's like a path with borders in the garden, they made you stay on the path and see all the lovely flowers. You had to stay in the bounds. If no borders were there one could wander about aimlessly and miss a lot the garden had to offer.

On the carriage ride home from church, Mother mentioned, "A nice young man, Isaac Peterson spoke to me. He asked permission to call on us Thursday morning at 10:00 a.m. He wants to bring his Grandmother Alicia Conrad to meet you. She was sister-in-law to your Grandmother Smythe. I told him that would be fine. I also told him they should plan to stay awhile and that we would enjoy their time with us."

Chapter 7

Thursday morning, the young women sat in Eva's room in front of the window. Elizabeth absentmindedly ran her fingers over the white velvet drapes that when closed kept out the intense heat or cold. She watched the lace sheers billow in and out with the breeze from the open space as they wondered about Grandmother Smythe's sister-in-law Alicia Conrad. Eva told Katherine what little she knew about her great uncle Barnabas Hamilton. The doctor and his wife had lived in France, with their daughter. She knew grandmother had visited them but not much more information except that Barnabas had died of the plague many years ago, at a young age. Since he was a doctor he would have been exposed over and over. His widow must have remarried, since her name was Conrad now.

Katherine smiled and her eyes shone as she

started their old childhood game where they guessed about their visitors. "Do you think Alicia will be ancient and wrinkled, straight nose or hooked, scary or saintly, nice or mean?" They both burst out laughing.

Mother came into the room smiling. "I heard what you said. I'm so glad I did. It sounds like the two of you growing up. I think you had the most fun together of any children I ever saw. Was that the visitor game?"

"Yes, it's still fun. I needed that laugh. Katherine wants to know if you want to have coffee or tea served when they arrive. Mother, what do you think?"

Sarah said, "Katherine, have both ready with the little cakes and cookies and finger sandwiches. I'll ask what they prefer and tell you which to serve. I know I want coffee. So, if you have both on the tray it will be a big help. The rolling cart will be needed to carry everything. I'm so glad you found it. I like the way it looks, and it makes us seem more elegant when you use it. Most homes still hand carry around those heavy trays. I think our guests will want something right away since they're coming all the way from Lenox Landing. Wilmerth and I were there a few times, it's a nice scenic place. The lake is a few miles from the mountains. Of course, the lake with the mountain view is breathtaking. We loved watching the sun rise and set on the lake with the reflection of the mountain on it. Oh, Katherine do you think any of the jelly roll cake was left? If there is, please add it to the goodies."

Eva said, "It was the best cake. My favorite was

the lemon filled one, but you couldn't fault the raspberry one. What will we ever do if we must replace Martha? I know she is training several of the girls, but I hope we don't have to face that problem any time soon. Mother did you know Doctor Webb is sweet on her?"

Sarah said, "That was just a joke. They both said so."

"No, Mother he told me Martha wanted true love and because he was nervous, he replied that he truly loved her cooking. I think he planned to ask her to marry him. When he didn't say it correctly, she got mad and made it into a joke. And he has had to live with his mistake all these years."

Sarah shook her head. "I didn't know."

"Isn't that the most tragic thing you've heard? Neither of them has married. Do you think we can get them together? But if we do that, we lose Martha for sure," Eva said.

Mother's eyes twinkled, as any good matchmaker's should. "Doctor Webb is about to retire. I don't think he has anywhere to go when he does. I don't think he has much money. Many people pay him with a chicken or fruits and vegetables. Martha is still able to work. Eva you brought up a good point that she may not be able to do it much longer. I hadn't ever thought about what we'd do if she wasn't here to cook for us."

Mother crossed over to a chair by Eva and sat down. The three were quiet for a few minutes all lost in her own thoughts. The view from this window was lovely, with the gardens, lawn, trees and some of the valley below laid out before them.

Eva clasped her hands and got up and hugged her mother. "I have an idea. The gate keeper's cottage is available, no one has lived there in a long time. We could fix it up for them."

Sarah thought about it. "Your Grandmother Smythe's room is comfortable and in another wing of the house. Martha wouldn't need to go out in the cold to get here in the mornings. When she retires, she can still give advice to the helpers and the doctor would be able to find things of interest to occupy his time. What do you think about that solution to the problem?"

Eva nodded. "Good idea. It will be nice to have them here."

Katherine joined the conversation, "We could have a wedding on the grounds for them. It would have been perfect to have it in the chapel. It's sad that lightning struck it and burned it down. Or maybe they would prefer the church in the village."

Eva frowned as the thought crossed her mind that maybe God had burned the chapel, so she wouldn't marry William in it. "Mother, that's positively wonderful, Grandmother's suite will be perfect for them. Now how do we bring them together?"

"Leave it to me. I'll have a talk with Doctor Webb and find out his true feelings then go from there. We had better get moving. Our guests will arrive soon. I sure have missed these bedroom chats. You two energize me so much." Mother turned, and a swirl of pink was all we saw. Katherine and Eva laughed again. She had missed so much fun while being married to William. He was always trying to get rid of Katherine. He didn't want Eva to have any friends. She didn't need to worry about his arguments any longer. Maybe in time she could forget he had tried to kill her. She had to get ready for company.

Her cream-colored dress lay out before her, she knew society dictated, a widow wears black only. She decided that today she would disregard it in her own home and wear the cream dress and add the tiger brooch with the emerald eyes her father had given her. She hoped no one would notice her breach of etiquette and hold it against her. She needed relief from the stress of the last week. In a day or two the dressmaker would deliver all the black clothes she was obligated to wear and would be seen in for the next year. She was dressed and ready.

Might as well go down and wait in the morning room with her mother. As she started down the wide staircase, she realized how lovely her surroundings were with the white walls and ornate smooth mahogany banister. The wood floors were beautiful, the chandelier magnificent in its size and delicacy. She always knew she loved their home, Amber Manor, but now she saw it with fresh eyes. All the things around her were more important once she had come so close to losing it forever.

Chapter 8

Tom, the doorman, announced the arrival of their guests. "Mr. Isaac Peterson and his Grandmother, Mrs. Alicia Conrad."

Isaac Peterson took Eva's breath away. She never saw anyone so handsome. Striking is how she described him. His hair shone platinum in the sunlight as he stood by the window. The platinum color that's so popular with dressmakers right now was the silky sheen of his hair and his eyebrows too. Hazel eyes and an easy smile made his face perfect. She noticed his sumptuous lips. *Oh, God,* she prayed, *keep this man away. I'm a widow*, she reminded herself. Goodness what was this? *Attracted to a man so soon after your husband died. What is going on with you?* Was she going completely crazy? She didn't want to go to an asylum. She looked again. He was tall. She didn't see anything about him that wasn't fine. His stylish suit was dark charcoal and perfectly tailored for him.

His grandmother Alicia Conrad was just as unusual as he. She was not as tall, but taller than most women. Her hair and eyebrows were the whitest white she had seen on an older woman. She'd probably had the platinum color too. Her wrinkles looked as if she smiled and laughed a great deal. She wore a lovely teal green dress with lace at the high collar and cuffs. The lace tapered over the top of her hand just short of her fingers, which were long and slender. Introductions were made, everyone was comfortably seated, and condolences were made for the loss of Eva's husband. Katherine brought in the trolley with refreshments.

Alicia said, "I prefer tea. Thank you for offering both. And yes, after that long trip, I'm a bit hungry." She selected her cakes and cookies. "Is Martha still your cook? I always loved her spice cookies. Of course I knew her mother, Ruthie who was the cook here before her."

Sarah was pleased and said, "Yes she is here and made these. I don't know how she had time for extra cookies for today, with all the cooking that was done for the funeral. She knew who was coming today so she might have made them for you. I'm glad you have been here before. We welcome you to our home."

Isaac filled his plate and had coffee with Eva and her mother. He said, "Grandmother has some things to give you Eva. Would you like to wait until your mother retires or do you mind if she hears the

68

events that have brought us here today? I'm sorry Mrs. Smythe, but I don't know how much you know about your mother-in-law's business. It's up to Miss Eva to decide."

She didn't want to hurt Mother's feelings, but she didn't know if she should hear all that must be revealed. Especially that Grandmother kept William from killing me. She thought awhile, many ideas raced around in her brain. "Mother there are some things I haven't told you that have happened in the past few days. I think we are going to get more shocks from the telling of Grandmother's secrets. You have always been truthful, so I depend on you to tell me if you want to stay and find out with me. And then hear what else I know. Can you do that comfortably?"

Mother said, "Of course, dear, I lived many years with Mary Beth. I probably know more about things than you think I would. I do want to know what Mrs. Conrad has to say."

Eva said, "Very well, we are ready to continue, Mrs. Conrad."

Alicia looked at each of them and started her story. "Your grandmother and I met as young girls. Her brother Barnabas had to take a horse to the livery in town. Mary Beth begged her father to let her go. He relented and allowed it. On the way, Barney was mad that he had to go and madder still that she had to come along. He was ranting about having to go see the devil himself. When she asked about it, he told her, "'You heard Old Preacher Potter, Sunday talk about the devil and how fire shot out of his eyes. I hear tell that blacksmith

Roberts is the devil. We go to church to worship God some people gather to worship the devil. Not sure how many devils there are or if there is just one. But he's one for sure. He must work at the forge because it's the only place hot enough for him around here.'"

Alicia sipped her newly poured cup of tea and continued. "Barney and Mary Beth were both scared by the time they got to the blacksmith shop. Their eyes were as big as saucers. Barney pushed the door open a bit wider. It creaked, and they trembled.

"The giant man was turning a horseshoe. His face was sweaty, dripping droplets on the ground. His huge arms and hands worked to create the angle he needed the iron to go to make it fit the horse. The heat from the forge was overwhelming even standing halfway out the door. The blacksmith plunged the horseshoe into water and instantly steam flew off it and made a sizzling sound. He looked up and smiled at each of them as he moved to the side bench for a towel and started wiping his face, neck and arms. He said "Hello, I'm Samson. What can I do for you today?"

Mary Beth moved behind Barney and peeked out from behind him. He nervously cleared his throat, "My father sent us to have this horse shod. He wants you to send the bill home with me and he will dispatch the overseer to pay it tomorrow."

"Just who might you be, young man?"

"I'm Barnabas Hamilton of Amber Manor." Barney had made himself stand as tall as he was able, as he spoke.

"In that case, I can help you. I have done much work for Mr. Hamilton of Amber Manor. Do you want to stay and watch me make the horseshoes?"

Barney wanted to stay but he was afraid. Dad always said to face your fears, so he had better stay, he decided. "Yes, it will be interesting to watch you make the horseshoes."

"Come over here and sit on the hay bales. Where are you, Alicia? Come out and introduce yourself to these nice children."

Barney stiffened and started to speak, "I'm not a child, I'm the man next in line to rule our house." But the sentence died on his tongue, when I stood up from behind a bale, the ones Samson had asked them to sit on. He looked me over good.

I thought he was the most handsome boy I had seen in my life. Tall, thin, but muscular, black eyes like his hair. His face was thin and long, like his nose. I smiled shyly and he smiled back but I saw him thinking, she is so young, and he dismissed me like a flower in the grass.

"I'm Alicia Thomason; I'm pleased to meet you both." I held out my hand.

"Barnabas Hamilton, you can call me, Barney. And this is my sister Mary Beth." Looking at the ground, he extended his hand and glanced at me. I smiled, showed my dimples and shook his hand, longer than was polite etiquette. Mary Beth held her hand out to be shaken so, I let go of Barney's and shook hers. We did all the usual questions and answers of new friends, while Samson worked on the horseshoes. First, he picked up each of the horses feet, measured them then started. It was so hot that we soon were heading outside. I lived a short way up the street, so we went there. I asked my mother for some lemonade. She said we could have some if we would take a glass to Samson first. We took it and the lunch she had made for him. When we got back, she gave us cookies too.

"Our house is not very big and when Samson comes for supper, he almost fills it up all by himself." I told them. We laughed and had a wonderful afternoon. It was time for supper when Samson was finished. He cleaned himself up and brought the horse to my house knowing the children would be there. He had a paper for Barney with the amount owed for the horseshoes. Mother invited him in for the evening meal with us when Mary Beth asked, "Are you the devil himself?"

Mother and Samson looked shocked; I couldn't imagine anyone being so rude. Barney shrunk down in size. Then Samson gave out his giant laugh. "Why would you think that, little girl?"

"Preacher Potter said you were the devil himself and had to stay at the forge to be hot like Hades. Are you really him? My brother said there are lots of Gods. Are there lots of Devils?" Samson laughed until tears came out of his eyes. He stopped and looked at Mary Beth and said in a very serious voice. "No child, I'm not the Devil. I'm a very good Blacksmith. I do have a bit of magic I'll share with you someday soon. You haven't a thing to be afraid of with me." He smiled and sent them on their way home and went in to eat with us."

Alicia sipped her cool tea. Mother took the cup and put the cold tea in the crockery canister and poured her a fresh cup of hot tea. She did the same for us with the coffee. We sipped it awhile. The cookies were passed again. Sarah asked her to continue the story.

Alicia said. "I'll be pleased to do so. It has been a long time since I have relived these cherished memories. My mother had been friends with Mary Beth's mother, so we were able to play together. Usually Barney would bring her to my house and pick her up or he would come down and bring me up here. Occasionally he would stay if we were going to do something that interested him, such as rock hunting, or gathering herbs for mother. She showed us which to pick and what not to touch. We all loved riding out across the fields. His excuse to stay with us was that we might need his protection. We liked having him along.

When I came here to play, Mrs. Hamilton wanted us to do cross stitch, or have cook teach us how to make something. We both liked doing those things, so it was fun to do it together. Cook would write down the recipe and give me a copy. Mary Beth then copied it for herself, so cook wouldn't need to write it two times. Her book with those recipes should be in the library. Have you seen it?"

Sarah started laughing. "You don't know how many times Mary Beth tried to teach them to me. Finally, I hid the book. I didn't realize she only had the book out for me. She knew them by heart. When she saw that I would go so far as to hide the recipe book, she gave up on me ever becoming a cook. We always had a cook and she made sure they had those recipes and she would take days when the cook only had to peel the carrots or potatoes and Mary Beth produced the meal. Oh, I miss her biscuits and breads. The house smelled so good when she was baking. Funny I usually don't even notice the baking smells now. Maybe it was knowing how good it would be and we anticipated eating it. She experimented and created recipes herself. We still use them today. She was a marvel in the kitchen. Perhaps it was Mary Beth making a production of it that was so much fun."

They all enjoyed this story of Mothers. Commented on it and Eva told them, "I have the Cookbook in a box in my room. Grandmother tried to teach me to cook too. I did pick up some of it and do it well enough we wouldn't starve, and the food would taste good, but I don't have the love of cooking like Grandmother did." she said, "Alicia please tell us more. This is fun."

Alicia said. "Yes, telling it in the safety of your warm home is enjoyable. The three of us had fun for a couple of years. Mary Beth and I were about two months apart in age and I was the oldest. Often during this time, we enjoyed digging in a mine on Samson's property where he allowed us to dig, he said with his work he didn't have time to do it. He told us we could keep anything we found. What an adventure. We made up stories to go with the days' work. One day we had been digging awhile and getting tired.

Barney said, 'I'm going to dig over here awhile. Alicia, you dig over here', and took me to a spot and did the same with Mary Beth. We were in a triangle, each digging by ourselves.

Mary Beth found a fantastic amber stone, just as she started to shout, so did Barney and I.

My find was a magnificent emerald and the stone Barney held up was a giant black onyx. We were all jumping up and down hugging each other and shouting.

"Be careful of the candles." Barney shouted, as mine tipped over. No one was hurt. I lit it again from Barney's, which he had sat on the ground carefully before jumping up. We decided to find the rest of the stones, surely there were more to be found. We didn't think in terms of greed. Just there should be others. We dug around a bit longer but never found anything else. We had been in the mine longer than usual, so Samson told us he came to investigate. He saw three happy youngsters jumping up and down shouting as we came out of the mine entrance.

Samson said, "I thought you were hurt when I got to the entrance and heard all the shouting. Why are you shouting? Come out here into the light and put out the candles."

Mary Beth got to him first. "Look what I found! This stone looks like our home."

"It sure does," he told her, 'the color of Amber Manor on certain days when the sun is right casts that color on the gray rock of your house. That's why old Bartholomew Neville your great-great-great grandfather I think, named the place he built AMBER MANOR. It's a sight to behold when it happens. I usually look to see. Do you pay attention to it?"

"Yes, Father is very proud that we have such a

beautiful place to live," Mary Beth said.

Barney nudged me forward. "Show Samson what you found Alicia."

I held out my hand, the sun hit the emerald and green light shone around us and on the ground.

"That's lovely too, like you, dear Alicia. Barney what did you discover?" Samson asked.

He brought forth the onyx.

"These are wonderful now but wait until you get them polished. Let us go make them better. Go to Alicia's house and I'll bring what we need to work with over there."

We were making so much noise as we ran over there that mother met us at the door. She opened it, "I thought a band of banshees was coming down the road. Who are you? Is this a pirate gang, or wild cutthroats? Do I dare let you into my house?" We were laughing so hard. She said "I don't guess that wild things would giggle so much. You had better come in before the neighbors think I'm tickling you with the feather duster." Once we had all trooped inside, she continued. "I have freshly baked light bread and milk, any takers?" She heard, "Me," "Me," "Me, please, ma'am." We were bouncing in our chairs with excitement. But we waited until she served us and sat down with us to start. She had placed a glass of milk and bread for Samson when I told her he was coming over too.

Samson arrived just as Mother sat down and she called for him to come in so we could say the prayer for our repast.

He said the blessing. "Have you shown Alicia's mother your treasures?"

"No, sir." Barney held his onyx out to her.

"Oh, where did you find it? It must be very valuable. I have never seen anything like it. What are you going to do with it?" she asked.

"Found it in the mine. Mr. Samson said it needs polishing. He was late so he could bring that box." Barney said.

Mother handed the onyx back to Barney.

I held out my emerald. The light from the candle on the table again made green shafts of color, on the tablecloth.

Mother had tears in her eyes. "That stone is beautiful I love the green light it gives off. Mary Beth, what are you holding in your hand?" she asked.

The amber was handed to her for inspection. "It's like the color that comes off your house I love to look at Amber Manor when the gray stones turn that color." She looked around the table and teasingly asked, "Where is mine? You have all three found treasure today. I was right when I asked if you were a bunch of pirates. Maybe this is part of the loot stolen from a great sailing ship come from halfway around the world. Samson, did you find any of these stones too?"

Samson said, "I didn't find any. I'll show these young people how to make them shine more than they already do. Then the fun of choosing what to make out of them starts. I have a big book of all kinds of designs for jewelry. We don't want you to carry around lumps of rock."

He looked at each of us and very seriously said, "You have found very precious gemstones. Like no other in the whole world. These are magical stones. You each found the one meant for only you. You must understand that the power inside them will be transferred to you when you have need of it. They hold valuable assets you will be able to use, healing ability, and mystical powers. This is important, they can't become a plaything. You have received them because you will need them to face your course in life. But with all the magical things there are people who will think you a witch or devil when they're used. Tell no one about the power they hold."

He thought for a few minutes, "Mary Beth, remember when you asked me if I was the devil? The preacher who said, Samson is the devil himself, had seen something miraculous that I had done. He attributed it to the devil, instead of seeing the glory of God in the event. I'm sad that he interpreted it incorrectly." He stood up and went to the box he brought into the house.

Mother got up and prepared the table for them to use, to polish the stones. Samson thanked her. He gave Barney and me some liquid poured on a nice soft cloth and showed us how to rub them. He was right, they were more dazzling than when we found them. Mary Beth was given a different kind of cloth with no oil on it. Samson explained to all of us that, "Amber is fossilized resin from ancient trees, over time it turns into rock. You know how the honey looking sap is on certain trees. In thousands of years, it will become amber. It scratches easily and is very delicate. Sometimes you will find a bug, dirt, or something caught inside the amber. This one is totally clear and about as perfect as you could ever find. You can never store it with your other jewelry, it must be kept separate. We shall find a way of protecting it." He was silent a few minutes.

Samson said, "I was thinking, trying to remember all I know about the powers of gemstones like the ones you found today. Amber's healing power is especially for the eyes and throat. Amber is to bring good luck. Also keeps your mind active, make the wearer look more attractive and balance your aggressiveness. It may have been one of the oldest substances used for human adornment."

"We are going to take your stones and create something you can wear and cherish all your life and pass on to your children and grandchildren. No one has ever had one like it. I'm excited to see what you want to make out of these stones. I'll tell you more about the stones as we go along. Are you ready to choose the design for your gems?"

"Yes, yes, yes." They all said at once.

He went to the box again and brought to the table a large book with all kinds of pictures drawn in it.

"What is it?" Alicia asked.

"These are designs of other jewelry. You will each pick several you like, and we will make something that includes the idea you like but making it a little different with something unique. Just for us. You shall become jewelry designers."

Mother and the rest of us gathered behind Samson's chair and looked over his shoulder at the gorgeous designs.

"I think the black onyx has to be a ring. Barney, you won't be able to wear it until you're a fully-grown man, so no one will question why a boy would have such a valuable ring. It will give you strength, courage and valor. But I'll arrange something so you can carry it always with you.

You must be very careful of it. It can scratch easily or chip off."

"What does my emerald do?" Alicia asked.

"The emerald brings truth and honor. An amulet for the girls, I think would be the best. Come, children. First, we create the ring for Barnabas." This is the first time he had called Barney by his given name, it sounded so dignified. We were at a threshold in our lives. Something important was happening right here today to all of us. Samson showed us drawings of many wonderful rings. Barney liked the lion head. Samson drew on a new paper a lion head on one side of the band with the onyx in the center and Barney's initials on the side opposite the lion head. Barney was amazed with joy. None of us had ever seen anything like it. This lion was better than the one in the book, the initials were elegant. Samson was smiling approvingly at his drawing. "I can see how he will go."

He looked at me right in the eye and asked. "Alicia, may I take a little of your emerald to make the eyes for the lion?"

I didn't want to do it, but Barney wanted it so avidly. He fidgeted trying to be prepared if I said no, I couldn't disappoint him. I looked at the others and they all nodded and wanted me to give some of my emerald for this magnificent ring to be even more beautiful.

"I, Alicia Thomason, give you, Samson Roberts, permission to cut the amount you need from my emerald for the eyes of the lion ring being made for Barnabas Hamilton." We all laughed at that formal pronouncement.

"Alicia, you have chosen a very noble action sharing your emerald with Barney." Mother said, and everyone agreed.

Samson said, "You have chosen well, boy. The lion has strength, and courage. The Onyx will scratch easily I'll build it up with the lion on one side and the initials on the other, the onyx will be set down a little. This black one has a wonderful luster and clarity. Onyx usually shows its bands of color, yours is taken between the bands making it pure color. This stone comes in many colors. This is a noble stone worthy of you and the design you have approved. That will make it uniquely yours. The emerald eyes will add to the Onyx's power to heal and let you seek out true friends. It needs a special name. When I give you the ring, after it's finished, I'll tell you the name of your ring."

"It's almost time for you to be heading home. Mrs. Thomason, do you mind if we meet here each day to plan and work on these gems?" Samson asked.

Mother looked at us and smiled. "Of course, you can, as long as I can feel like I'm part of this great adventure. It feels like we are going on a crusade or a quest."

Samson said "How right you are, fine lady. It's a quest. These youngsters will have challenges and I aim to help them be ready, when the time comes. This ring for Barnabas and the girls' amulets will make them know they can face anything in life. The power of the items is only usable if the owner knows they're there. They won't grant wishes such as I want a new horse or that coat I saw in the dressmaker's window. They're for personal protection," he told my mother, but he watched us to make sure we understood what we had in these precious gifts we would receive. We decided to meet at 11:00 a.m. and have dinner at my house and work until suppertime.

Barney and Mary Beth went home, and Samson stayed to supper with us. He could see how excited we were about our project, but he had warned all of us to keep this business our secret. It was going to be hard to do. How do you keep quiet about something this unusual and important? The next day we were ready to start. The box was here waiting for Samson to arrive. When he came in with a smile, we reflected it back to him. Mother told him to sit down and have a cup of coffee. She gave us a mug of hot cocoa. Her cocoa was the best, she gave us each a big cookie and Samson ate another one before we got to work for the day.

"We have a design for the ring, now the girls need to decide what they want for their very own. Oh, before we open the dream book again, I need to ask Barney to do something for me. You girls can start looking at the book." He opened it and laid it on the table. "This volume is very old and easily torn. Please don't turn the pages until I come back so I can do it. Barney, come outside with me please."

Samson asked, "Is your father's hand bigger than yours? We are talking about his ring finger. There is a chance your hand could get bigger, but I don't think so. Let me look at it." He inspected the young man's hand. "Have you tried on any of his rings lately?"

Barney blushed, hung his head, and muttered, "Yes. I only wanted to see if it would fit and it did. Father would be mad if he knew, we are never to touch our parent's belongings, it's bad manners."

"I need you to take a piece of paper and lay the ring on it and trace around the inside of the ring. I'll measure your finger and check it with the paper trace and see how accurate it is so we can make it fit well, so you can wear it comfortably with ease. Bring it along as soon as you are able."

"I will." They went back to the house and the girls.

Alicia moved out of the chair in front of the book so Samson could sit in it. He sat and we looked at the pages as he turned them for us. I saw a wreath of laurel leaves I really liked, a quill feather, maple leaf and several other nice shapes. "I want leaves to compliment the green of new beginning life in the earth. Could it be a tree of life?" I ran into my room and brought out an old quilt my grandmother had made with the tree of life pattern on the top. It was a giant tree with leaves with names embroidered of her family, my name was on it too. We looked at it and Samson told us more about the properties of the emerald and said, Life is one of the attributes of the stone. Alicia you have the idea I had in mind. How do you think we could create it?"

"We need gold leaves or branches. Like the laurel leaves crown wreath. Maybe you could take the gold leaves and bring them around the edges and up a little on top of the emerald, if it was set like this?" I moved the emerald at an angle on the table and traced with my hand where I thought the leaves could fit.

"How about a tree trunk with branches and leaves, twining around with the angle you showed me?"

"That would be perfect." I clasped my hands in delight.

"Alicia pick out the kind of chain you like, and we will see what we can come up with for your amulet."

I took my time looking and finally found the one I decided was perfect. "Will this one last a hundred years?"

Everyone was laughing at me.

"It should. Alicia your choice is complementary to the whole necklace you have described. You and Barney, and Mary Beth look for the design for the amber, while I draw." Samson said.

I couldn't keep my mind on Mary Beth's design while he was about to draw my very own masterpiece. I wondered how he learned to draw so beautifully. I didn't want to ask and disturb his flow onto the paper.

He took out a paper and started to draw. First, he drew an ancient gnarled tree trunk, then the branches. He drew the shape of my stone, one big piece of emerald. Next came the twining branches with little leaves coming up around the edges and a couple of them along the side edge. When the design was ready Samson handed it to me.

I cried when I saw it and so did my mother. Barney and Mary Beth were awed. "This is so much better than I had imagined," Alicia said.

"That will be the most beautiful necklace I have ever seen," Mother said, then announced it was time for dinner. We moved everything off the table. Mary Beth and I sat the table and we had Samson say the prayer. Mother's beans and cornbread with sliced onions and tomato, apple pie and milk to drink made us a hearty noontime meal. After we ate, Mary Beth and I hurried to clear the table and wash dishes so we could get back to her amber design. Five of us in our small kitchen was a bit crowded, but no one was concerned about it. It was cozy with the fireplace and fragrant herbs, hanging in the mudroom as you entered the door. Good food scents mixed with the herbs soothed the soul.

Mother generated the joy of life that kept us happy, and we laughed at little things. Like the time mother was hanging out laundry and the young hawk swooped down for one of our chickens and got to tangle with the rooster who was behind the spring house when the ruckus started. The rooster had some minor damage, but the hawk knew he had been in a fight. Mother called us to come outside. We all flapped our arms and yelled at the hawk. When the big bird flew off all of us sat in the grass, we laughed so hard, at how funny the others looked trying to shoo it away.

Back to the work we went. Mary Beth chose a twined three strand chain that looked delicate. "I want the world with the amber inside." She took a paper and drew her idea.

Samson drew it on another paper, and it was wonderful. "I would have a friend blow a glass ball around your amber. I would make the stone stationary inside, so it doesn't hit the glass. Then wrap the chain around the glass in about five strands from top to bottom, put a jeweler's loop to hold it and attach it to the chain. The mesh like look of the thin chains intertwined will be delicate in appearance but it will be strong.

"Mary Beth glowed and kissed and hugged Samson for the way he took her idea and created such an unusual item that would be her own. She and Barney went home after the designs were all selected. Everyone was exhausted. Samson ate with mother and me again. We sure enjoyed his presence."

Alicia sipped more tea and said, "My throat is dry, it's been awhile since I talked this much." She continued the story.

It took about a month for all the designs to be finished. Sampson had a jeweler friend and a glass blower help with certain things. At last they were ready. Samson and Mother made a big formal unveiling ceremony. It was so exciting. Mary Beth and Barney told their mother that my mother was making us a formal high tea. Barney was dressed in his dark blue suit that made his brown eyes darker and he looked so handsome to me. Mary Beth wore her creamy white dress with the soft ruffles around the sleeve. She looked elegant the candlelight made the cream-colored silk shimmer. I had on my white lace dress.

Mother wore her light-yellow Sunday dress.

Samson was dressed in his black meeting suit. We had placed laurel leaves across the mantel with two large candles lighted in the center. The table was set for the high tea. Our china Mother had inherited was set out on the white linen tablecloth, with the matching napkins folded beside the plates. Her silver that we rarely used was on full display. A small rosebud vase was placed on the left of the plate above the forks. Each vase had a tiny fairy rose of pink and a couple of yellow dandelions. Our house smelled like baked goods and flowers. We had picked white Carnations and red, pink and yellow roses then put them in two big vases. Party excitement filled our cozy home.

Mother had made little sandwiches with cucumber, some with ham and some with watercress, and her special egg salad. She made a small fresh fruit salad, tiny thumbprint cookies with preserves in the print from our thumb. We put peach in some and strawberry in the others. Petit fours with the hard white and some with hard chocolate frosting. The fudge was out of this world and divinity too. We had two kinds of tea. A black oolong tea from China, and an English tea from India. Some time was spent trying to figure out how it could be English tea if it came from India. Wonderful food, great conversation and anticipation about the unveiling of the gems sent the time flying down the day.

Finally, Samson got up from the table and went to the counter while Mother cleared the dishes and everything from the table. She sat one of the mantle candles in the center of the table. She sat down and

Samson lifted a kitchen towel off the covered cake dish, he had put on the table.

Under the towel were three black velvet pouches. His big hand dwarfed the foot on the cake plate. He put a black bag before each of us. "Don't open them until I tell you to do it."

Mary Beth, Mother, and I had stitched a bag to conceal the gems in our undergarments. It was a small taffeta bag made like an envelope that had a buttonhole in the flap and one in the front and back of the pocket, the corresponding button went through the three buttonholes. Large buttons had been sewn onto our petticoats and mother had sewn them inside Barney's underwear waist. We had sewn extra pockets to be washed with the undergarments, so the servants could be told, "We wanted to make sure we didn't lose anything, it was a nice idea to have a space if you ever needed to use it. That way they wouldn't question why we put buttons on everything.

Samson started the formal celebration. "Barnabas, your Onyx is now named, THE RING OF VALOR. Wear it well. It has powers to make you full of courage and have faith in yourself. You will be well spoken, honor, courage and valor surround you and flow within. You may open your pouch and put the ring on your finger."

Barnabas did so. He finally spoke after clearing his throat a few times. "Thank you, Samson, my ring is very special. Please accept my gratitude. I feel as if I can do anything I set my mind to do. This is uplifting and humbling at the same time."

Mother held out her hand. "Barnabas, come

around the table to each of us and show off the details of your ring. Oh, Samson your ideal drawing was nice. What you have created here is so much more than we could have imagined," Mother commented as she turned Barnabas' hand in different directions to inspect the whole ring.

"Alicia what do you think?" Barnabas asked. He held out his hand to show to me the ring.

"The lion and the black onyx is wonderful, but the emerald eyes make him perfect. I'm so glad Samson thought of that and it came out so well. Black, gold, and emerald green should always be your colors if you ever have a flag or horse colors. This ring would be the perfect crest." I reluctantly let go of his hand. In all the excitement of the moment maybe he hadn't noticed the thrill that ran through me when his hand touched mine.

"Oh, Barnabas, this ring is elegant and just right for the man you're becoming. I can see you, my brother as a man of valor and courage. I'm so happy for you." Mary Beth reached up and kissed him.

Her actions sent shivers of jealousy up my spine. His sister could kiss him, but I couldn't. Next, it was my turn to see the emerald turned into a beautiful amulet.

"Alicia, your emerald is now called THE EMERALD OF TRUTH. It will help you know true friends and will discern false people. Health will be yours as well as love," Samson said.

My mouth opened but no words came out. It was exquisite. The golden trunk of the tree of life was heavy enough that the big emerald didn't overwhelm it. Lines in the gold made it look like a true to life tree. The shape of the emerald with the golden branches on it looked real too. I got up and went around the table and hugged Samson. I could see his happiness. "How can you make such beauty? I saw a lovely stone, but you brought it to life."

"We don't know how God allows us to be able to do certain things, but he will show us all what we can do if we look for our talents. Turn around Alicia and I'll clasp the pendant for you." Samson said. He held me away from him and looked at his achievement. "It is perfect Alicia."

I went around the table showing my amulet. Barnabas was close enough I could smell his breath and feel it on my neck.

He surprised me by saying, "The necklace is almost as beautiful as you are, Alicia Thomason."

Everyone laughed and agreed. I was flattered.

Mary Beth opened her velvet bag. "It's my turn, I can't wait any longer." She gasped at the amulet in her hand. "Mine is the most precious. I shall cherish it forever. Thank You, Thank You, Thank You, Samson!" She ran around the table and hugged him as tears ran down her face.

"Yours is very special I have added extra enchantments on it. You will have need of protection most of your life. It won't be the easiest life, but it will be fulfilling. You will be a strong woman and have enemies. You will have many friends too. Choose them carefully. A false friend can be treacherous. Your amber is now the Amulet of Safety, for it will bring you to safety. I predict an interesting full life. Turn around and let me put it on you. Then you can show everyone," Samson told Mary Beth.

He connected the clasp and she showed her amber stone inside its globe. It lay perfectly on the cream-colored dress and set it off perfectly.

Samson had started to say something when mother cut him off. "No, Samson, it's not over we have a gift for you. Compared to these wonderful items you have made it will amount to very little, but we wanted to have a surprise for you. Wait right here."

She went into the bedroom and brought out our offerings. A belt, from Barney, Mary Beth made handkerchiefs with his initials. I made him socks. Mother gave him a new white Sunday shirt she had made. He was truly surprised and happy with our meager gifts made with love.

Samson stood and said, "This has been a special day for all of us. Thank you for the gifts you have given me. We now must honor the gracious woman who made all this possible. By feeding us and letting us use her home. It's only fitting that she should open her gift right now." He handed her a velvet bag from his coat pocket.

Eyes wide with delight she opened it to find a beautiful chain that had a large gold heart with a little smaller heart shaped green jade in the center. Tears of joy were falling from those big brown eyes. She said, "Samson, it's too much. How could you know? I once saw a green jade and loved it. I never imagined I would ever own one. Thank you from the bottom of my heart." I noticed mother looked at him with love. This was not the first time

I had seen that look.

"Mrs. Thomason, I would like to speak in front of these witnesses. I have been in love with you for many years. I was afraid to speak to you about it. Since we have been working on this project, we have all been very close together like a family. Would you do me the honor of becoming my wife?" Samson asked.

Mother smiled and tears fell. "I love you too. I had almost given up on you ever asking me! I thought you might not feel the same since so much time went by, year after year. I would be honored to be your wife."

Samson moved over to her, took her in his arms, brought her to his body, and kissed her. I don't think any of us had seen such a long loving kiss before this one. It's a shock to see your mother responding to a man this way. We still had many things to learn, about everything in life.

Chapter 9

Katherine entered the room and waited for Alicia to finish her last sentence.

"Dinner is ready in the dining room, madam," Katherine announced formally. She grinned at Eva and she almost started to laugh out loud, but controlled herself.

Sarah said, "Katherine please show our guests where they may freshen up and then show them to the dining room."

"Yes Miss Sarah."

Eva said "Alicia, your story has delighted us. I hope we can resume it after our mid-day repast. Mr. Peterson it's a pleasure to have you with us today also, we shall see you next in the dining room." She got up and he stepped the distance to her and kissed Eva's hand. He had touched her again and it was brief, the mere brush of his lips on her hand, but it seared right through her.

He looked totally nonchalant. He must kiss every woman's hand. Mine was only one in the long line. I wonder if all the others have felt the special spark that went through me. Lord what is wrong with me? It's only been a short time since William died, it's not proper behavior for a young widow, or one of any age.

Eva watched Katherine lead Alicia and her grandson Isaac out to the prepared rooms. Mother had been silent as Alicia told the story. She had closely observed her daughter and saw her reaction to Isaac Peterson's kiss on her hand. She spoke, "I think you will be fine. I was so worried, but some of the sparkle has come back to your lovely brown eyes. I learned as a young girl that we shouldn't speak ill of the dead. I do however believe that William was not very nice to you. Eva, I want you to know I love you and you can always talk to me and if I can do anything to help you, I will. I hope you have always known that."

"Yes, Mother, I love you too. I am so glad you are my mother. Remember when you came to my room in the evenings and brushed my hair for one hundred strokes? I cherished those times. Even when you bopped me on top of my head with the wooden brush and told me to sit still. Then you tucked me into bed with a story and a goodnight kiss. I had a good childhood."

Patricia, a cook's assistant, came in to let them know that Katherine was taking the guests down.

Eva and her mother followed her to the dining room; and were already seated when Alicia and

Isaac arrived.

After dinner, Alicia requested time to rest before she resumed her story. Katherine took her to her room. Isaac had declined, saying he was used to travel and didn't need to rest. "Mrs. Smythe, Mrs. Davis, would you like to walk around outside awhile? It's a lovely day. I noticed you have a rose garden with some rather unusual plants." He gestured toward the door.

They took their shawls out of the closet by the door. Eva told Katherine where they were going, and they moved out into the daylight. They walked down the wide front steps. Eva breathed deeply and brought the fresh air into her body. It was exhilarating. She felt happy and full of hope.

The garden tour was grand. Her mother pointed out all the fauna and flora. Isaac was quite knowledgeable, and the conversation flowed easily. Eva enjoyed drinking in the sunlight and cool sweet air. Her mother had brought along her flower basket and shears. Isaac helped her cut a vase full of blossoms.

As they walked and shared a pleasant time together, her mind jumped back a few days.

William was being nice to her as they walked in the sunshine. They talked and laughed and enjoyed themselves. She was totally unprepared for the horrible feeling of being pushed off her fast horse and having been lifted upright and put back into the saddle. With the force of the hands holding her, she had expected bruises. None had appeared. He had to have been an Angel of God. The Amulet of Safety may have been responsible for calling him and

Grandmother, but it was a powerful hand that kept her from falling to her death. She had praised God ever since.

Her mother's voice cut into her thoughts and stopped her from reliving the nightmare. "Eva, come back to us. You look faint, talk to me please."

Not realizing Isaac was at her side and holding her arm in his to keep her from falling, she answered, "I'm fine Mother, just thinking about William." She didn't add *and his attempt to murder her. Or that a big angel saved her and her grandmother's ghost scared William and his horse, causing William's death.*

She had married a man who tried to murder her. Had he done it before? Maybe he had gotten away with it in his past, before he met her. What a sickening feeling, knowing someone wanted you dead. Perhaps it was different if it was a stranger who tried to kill you. But her husband, the man she married for life? Then the phrase hit her, *until death do us part.*

They were back in the parlor. Her mother handed her a small glass of sherry.

"Cognac, please, I can't abide Sherry." Eva said.

"I know that, sorry Eva. I wasn't thinking straight. You frightened me." Mother said.

Eva stammered when she could breathe again after the burning in her throat from the cognac. "Mr. Peterson, what ever must you think? I apologize for my behavior."

"You haven't a thing to apologize for, Madam. You're a new widow and it's to be expected that you would be affected by your surroundings and people imposing on your hospitality. Grandmother thought this time was when you needed to hear what she had to say. If you like we can leave as soon as Grandmother wakes up."

"That would greatly distress me sir. We are enjoying Alicia's story very much. It's painful to be grieving at a time when I have an opportunity to learn more about my own grandmother. If it is too awful for you to remain in my presence, then I'll understand. But my hope is that you will continue with us for several more days," she said, and hoped she didn't sound like she was begging.

"Since you desire it, we will stay. Thank you. I noticed Grandmother's knees are hurting her and she was rubbing her hands when she talked earlier. She won't mention it, but she is in great pain. It comes and goes. Some days she can outwalk me, and some she can hardly move. I believe that's her reason to visit currently. She may think there won't be another chance to come before her health gets worse. She did want to come here to see the place again. She and Mary Beth spent a good deal of their lives running in and out of here. Grandmother mentioned she wanted to see the house shaded in the amber glow she remembers so well. I hope it happens while we are here. That would make her happy. I want to see it too. She gives such a beautiful description of the sight," Isaac said.

"It happens often, I'm sure you will get to see it," Sarah said.

Alicia had rung the bell for Katherine, and she had helped the older woman down the stairs. Katherine brought her directly to the table and seated her. Then she came to us and announced, "Supper is ready. I have taken the liberty of taking Mrs. Conrad directly to the dining hall. I was sure that would be fine with you Mrs. Smythe."

Sarah nodded her approval. We followed Katherine to the dining room for our evening meal. Cook out did herself. She made meat pies with pot roast, potatoes, carrots, onions, and corn in them. The crust was flaky and delicious. We also had green beans, sliced tomatoes, lettuce, cucumbers in vinegar, and for dessert she had made vinegar pie. Martha won several blue ribbons at the county fair for her pies. Her ribbons and plaques were displayed in a beautiful case on the kitchen wall. We were all pleased with the hearty meal.

Alicia said, "This is the same supper we were served many of the times I ate here. Ruthie tried to teach my mother how to make the meat pies. She never learned to do it right. We had some tasty misses, but it never was the same as Ruthie's. Vinegar pie was my favorite too. Mary Beth could make it, though. I didn't ever learn to make it correctly. Being here brings back so many wonderful memories."

Chapter 10

They moved back to the parlor and had tea and coffee. They were ready to hear more of the story about Alicia, Mary Beth, and Barney. Alicia started. "I don't know how much of the story you already know, what your family history reflects or how to tell some of the happenings. If you're agreeable, I think it would be advisable to read it aloud from Mary Beth's diaries. Isaac has a good strong voice and I would like for him to be the reader. Do you agree? Mary Beth gave me the diaries for safe keeping to be given back to you, Eva, when the time was right. She trusted me to know when that time would be right. I deem it to be now. I think there was more to the death of your husband than we have heard and that The Amulet of Safety was used."

Mother gasped. "No, that's not possible. How

could the Amulet be needed when your husband was the one in danger? Eva, did you try to use it to save him? Isn't it lost?"

Eva hung her head a minute and prayed for the right words to use. She sat up straight and stated firmly, "I believe we should have Isaac read Grandmother's journals. We will learn what we need to know about the amulet and her life. Then we can question the recent happenings. I have the amulet safe and will tell it later."

Alicia spoke, "Yes, my dear. Your grandmother told things well and it spared none of us. It all becomes clear as the readings advance."

"Mother, what do you think about reading them aloud?" Eva asked.

"Mary Beth told me bits and pieces. I don't think it will be such a shock, and that we can handle whatever we hear. And you have had, it appears an incident with the Amulet, I see no reason why everyone in the room shouldn't hear the story from Mary Beth herself."

"It's decided then. Isaac will you honor us with the reading?" Eva asked.

"It will be my pleasure to read Mary Beth (Hamilton) Smythe's diaries to you."

"BOOK ONE: Life of Mary Beth Hamilton

Dear Diary, it seems odd to address a book Dear Diary! I have had this book for ages, I don't know how long. I guess two or three years ago, given to me, for a birthday or holiday where gifts were exchanged. I hunted all over before finding you. What has happened is so out of this world that I must write it down.

Today was the unveiling of the most magnificent gift anyone could ever own. It's mine. I shall cherish it forever. A big party was held at Alicia's house. Her mother is the best. My mother is nice, but thinks of us as babies. I'm sure she likes us but Alicia's mother gushes over us like we are the most wonderful children in the world, like she does Alicia. She also acknowledges we are growing up.

The party was wonderful. Samson the blacksmith let Barney, Alicia and me, dig in his mine for several weeks, and then we found precious gems. He said, "They belong to you now, you found them. Let us make something special out of them."

What did he mean? They were special just as we found them. We couldn't believe our eyes when he showed us a book of designs and helped each of us to create our own pattern. He took our ideas, as impossible as they were and made them spectacular. Alicia's mother Mrs. Thomason, says, "Samson is a creative genius and great artist."

Our Father doesn't know about the artist. All he sees is his abilities as a blacksmith who makes harness, horseshoes and tack.

The Thomason house smelled so good and looked festive. A lace tablecloth and napkins covered the table and it was set with the best dishes and silver. Alicia's mother had made a High Tea. The food was wonderful, but it was hard to eat since we wanted to get to the unveiling of our gems.

It took Samson over a month to make the treasures we received. We had waited a long time already. He made me wait until last to open mine.

Barney was first. Samson called him Barnabas. It was so formal and made Barney seem and act older. You should see the black onyx with a lion's head with emerald eyes leaning onto the black and wrapped around the side of this ring. Opposite the lion are Barney's initials in scroll letters. Samson named it, "The Ring of Valor." Of course, Barney thinks his ring is the best of all the jewels Samson made. Brothers... God must have made them so sisters could suffer.

Next Alicia opened her emerald, made into a necklace with a golden tree base and golden leaves coming across the large emerald stone. Samson named it, "The Emerald of Truth". It's perfect for her. And of course, she thinks she got the special one.

Finally, my reveal. Samson named mine, Amulet of Safety. He put extra protective spells on it for me. Mine is the greatest of course. The amber stone is in a large glass globe surrounded by five chains coming up from the bottom to clasp on top, to the beautiful triple chain necklace. Maybe they're so special because we each think we got the nicest one Samson made.

We gave Samson some small gifts but nothing like what he has done for us. He had a green jade and gold heart necklace for Alicia's mother. I guess she thinks she got the finest one, too. After giving it to her, he asked her to marry him. Then right in front of us. He kissed her on the mouth and was leaning against her body holding her with his big arms wrapped around her. He kissed her for a long time.

She had said she would marry him and loved him too, before the kiss. But after it she would have had to marry Samson. It would be the only decent thing to do.

I wonder if father ever kissed our mother like that. Do married people do that? I don't know anyone to ask about these things. Growing up is hard at times like this. How do we find out?

Before we left for home Samson made us put them back into the black velvet pouches and pull the drawstring. Then we had to put them into the pockets we made to attach them, to our underskirts and to Barney's drawers. Mrs. Thomason had helped us make them. A button is sewn to the undergarment and there are three buttonholes in the pocket, one on the back and front of the pocket and one matching on the flap. You put what you want to carry in the pocket and put the button through all three buttonholes. It's a bit of work but we are carrying precious gems. Samson warned us about highwaymen and robbers that would like to get their hands on such a find.

These gems will always be worn on our person. Samson put selected spells on them for our health and protection. Barney thinks its superstition. But Samson is a fearsome man and I think he is good. It would be unfair, if we didn't believe him when he has been so kind and wonderful to us.

Dear Diary,

A few days have passed. My Amulet is safe. One of the laundry girls, Mattie, asked me today about the button on my petticoat below the waist. I showed her my lawn cloth pocket, that Mrs. Thomason had me create for such a time as this. We made ones that could go through the wash. And carry small stuff of little importance. Luckily, I had put a seashell and smooth stone in it. I told Mattie it was for my valuables and she liked the idea and wondered if she could make one to carry her special items.

I'll teach several of our young girls to make the pockets tomorrow afternoon. The idea caught on quickly, I cut out twenty pockets from the lawn cloth and got the buttons and thread ready for the class. Imagine, me a teacher, ha, ha.

Dear Diary,

It's about a week later than last entry. The Class went well as the girls could sew better than me and faster. Some of the other help saw what we were doing, looked over my pattern and everyone now has a pocket and button below their waistband. Mrs. Thomason laughed and thought it was nice to have started a new style. Even if no one knew, she had thought of it. Samson told her she should sell the idea to her dressmaker friend. Today she did. She got some money and will receive a commission on each petticoat purchased with it. The dressmaker also gave her a special wedding dress for her idea. Now fashionable ladies will be using the Thomason Button Pocket.

Samson told her, "You're now a real businesswoman."

She beamed at him.

I'm so happy for her and Samson. They both

seem very happy. It must be true love. Alicia says she has seen them looking at each other for years but each kept their distance until we found the gems, and all started working together to create beauty. She said they started to grow closer together. She is glad Samson will be her stepfather.

I wonder if I'll ever find my true love. I want someone romantic and suave. Handsome would be good but not a must. Maybe he will be mysterious, a bit older than me, thwarted by another and will live only for me. Sigh."

Chapter 11

Isaac sipped his coffee then continued.

"Dear Diary,

It has been around six months since I wrote on these pages. Life has us doing normal everyday events. I have enjoyed the time, but each day doesn't need a record. Several months ago, father started to act out of sorts. Everyone noticed but no one knows what was wrong. Maybe he was sick. Mother said to stay away from him, so we all did that.

Today I went to market with Etta, one of the cook's helpers. I like going with her. She knows how to choose the best fruit and melons, fresh meat and ripe tomatoes, and vegetables. We stood beside a booth with all kinds of nice items. Umbrellas, gloves, hats, knives, fancy cups and saucers and many other trade goods.

I heard Barney shout, "Mary Beth and Etta, get to Samson now!"

We both turned to go to Samson. A big hand reached out and grabbed my arm. I screamed and clutched the amulet under my skirt as the huge man pulled me up against his chest. I said, "Safety now!" The man growled at me.

Barney shouted, "Unhand her you brute! That's my sister. Let her go now." his voice was so forceful. He ran up and hit, the fellow who held me, in the nose. His grip was loosened and hands around my waist lifted me up in the air and moved me to the side. I grabbed an umbrella from the booth and hit the brute in the back with the sharp tip. Blood spurted on my dress. Then the other man holding a gun started yelling and pointed the gun at Barney. A shot was fired. I saw Barney lifted as I had been, and the shot totally missed him. The man with the gun fainted. The first one looked like he was dead as he hit the ground. The man at the booth shouted about evil spirits. Barney and I ran to Samson when we saw him coming toward us.

Etta had reached him, and he came as fast as he could. He took us back to Mrs. Thomason where he had sent Etta. Mrs. Thomason cleaned Barneys wounded hand, and put something on it that smelled awful. She then cleaned the blood off my dress.

Samson said, almost to himself, "I wonder how many others saw what I did?" He cleared his throat. "Barney, I saw you lifted off the ground and set out of the way of that bullet. Tell me what you felt, thought, and saw, everything that happened, please."

"Yes, sir," Barney said. "I didn't know the girls were in town shopping. I played cards at the inn when the man with the gun came in and told the brute, "I just saw the Hamilton girl in the marketplace with another girl. Let's grab her and make her father pay for what he did and give us money to get her back."

I followed them into the street. I had no weapon. I touched the ring at the side of my waist and said. "I need courage and strength."

I yelled at the girls, "Run to Samson." They both started to run. Etta got away but the brute caught Mary Beth and she screamed. I ran and hit him in the nose, I think it broke. She got loose and hit him in the back with an umbrella when he was about to hit me. He started to fall, and I saw the gun in the other man's hand. I saw the bullet coming at me. It would have hit and killed me. Big hands on my waist moved me off the ground and set me out of the path of it. Sampson, I thought you moved me, until I saw you coming toward us as we ran to you. When I saw both men on the ground, they looked dead. That scared me more than when they attacked. I heard the booth man yell but didn't know what he said." Barney paused. "Thank you, Samson, for your help. I was so scared. I didn't know what to do."

I jumped up and said, "You did everything just right! Your voice was forceful and had authority. When you told us to move, we didn't waste a second asking why. We started to move. You were brave and courageous. You called on your ring and I called on my amulet. We were miraculously saved. You had to have believed in the power or it wouldn't have worked for us. You may have saved my life." The next minute I was hugging him.

"Etta thank you, for doing as told and going to bring Samson to us," I said.

Etta looked badly shaken over the event but nodded her head up and down in acknowledgment of the compliment I had given her.

Samson said, "Etta, you have heard some things here today. You must not pass them as gossip. These men were evil to try to snatch Mary Beth. The talismans mentioned are for good not evil. If people knew about them there could be far reaching circumstances. Do you understand?"

Etta nodded.

Samson said, "I must have your sacred oath that you won't tell about the talisman or of the children lifted by mighty beings. You will have to tell about the ruffians trying to kidnap Mary Beth and how Barney was strong and brave and saved her. If asked you don't know anything else since you did as you were told and ran to bring help to them. There will be talk of demons and evil. But you will know better than to believe that. Do you so swear, Etta?"

Etta lifted her hand and said, "Sir, I, Etta Patton, do swear to this Oath." She gave a half smile.

Mrs. Thomason made us tea and brought us freshly baked cookies. It was comforting. We started to calm down when a knock came on the door. We all jumped a little at the sound. Samson said, "That will most likely be the constable." He looked at Barney and me. "You will know what to say. Don't worry. Etta, remain quiet." He got up and opened the door. It was the constable followed by a small crowd, growing larger by the minute. Many including the booth owner tried to crowd in. "Hi Samson, you have a couple of kids here who were in a fight in town?"

Samson allowed him inside, keeping the others out as he closed the door. "I have three scared young ones who had a terrible ordeal on their shopping trip."

"I have two dead men who were just taken from the street to the undertaker. What happened to them? The vendor says demons came up from out of the ground and protected these children. That they're the devil's spawn. Many in the crowd want to believe him. May I talk to them?"

Samson said, "I have sent for Mr. Hamilton. Maybe he should be here when you question them. If it was your boy and girl, you would want to be present for such an ordeal in their lives."

"Well if the vendor is right, their father would be the devil himself. Wouldn't he?" he smiled. "Neither of us believes that, so we'll wait for him."

I observed Alicia as she held Barney's hand.

Alicia's mother gave the constable cookies and tea.

We knew when father arrived from all the commotion outside. Samson hurriedly opened the door just enough to let him inside and not let anyone else scamper past him as some tried to do. Father moved to us and guardedly hugged us both at the same time.

"What did you do that brings a lynch mob?" he asked.

"Barney saved my life because he is so brave and good and valiant." I said all too loudly.

Father was stunned. Samson helped him sit down in a chair. "Tell me about it," he said when his composure had been regained.

Barney told father he had heard the men say they wanted to get back at him for what he had done to them. They were going to grab me and ransom me back to him. That he was mad and needed to protect his sister. He ran into the stall area and broke the nose of the man that held me and I was loosed. Then we both ran for Samson who rushed to us, because Etta had gotten away and sent him after us.

"That sounds good," the Constable said. "But how did the bad guys both die?"

"We were running away. I don't know how they died," I said.

"Me either," said Barney.

And that was the truth. We probably will never know how they died.

Father asked the Constable, "Were they the two, you arrested for robbing me awhile back?"

"Yes, Mr. Hamilton, they were the ones. They got out of jail a couple of days ago. I guess as you heard on the way, the booth owner is telling people demons came out of the ground to help the children. You will probably have repercussions from that lot. The ones who want to believe in evil instead of good." He shook his head. "Please wait here awhile until I can get the crowd to go home."

The constable went out and we could hear the noisy group get louder as the merchant inflamed them with his devil's spawn talk.

Father told Barney how proud he was of him taking care of his little sister. Then he spoiled the praise, when he noticed Alicia still held his hand, and frowned.

On the way home, father and son battled over Alicia, since she wasn't of their class and that Barney knew better than to hold her hand."

Chapter 12

Turning another page, Isaac shifted in his chair.

"Dear Diary,

Long time since I wrote in this book. Father is mad at me. He says I keep getting myself into messes. It has been about three and a half years since we met Samson. Today was the date set for his wedding to Mrs. Thomason. Alicia was the Maid of Honor and I was a Bridesmaid. We were at the church early so we would be in on all the activities.

The bride's dress was lovely and just right for her. It was part of her payment for the Thomason Button Pockets. The seamstress was doing very well with them and commissions are still being paid regularly. She had also been given some scraps of famous dresses so Mrs. Thomason could make

Alicia and I our dresses. Mrs. Thomason was dressed, and we all were waiting for the music to start. One of the church women came in and told us there was a slight delay.

"Mrs. Thomason, can I ask a question. If you think I'm bad for asking, please tell me you do not want to answer it."

"Mary Beth you can ask what you want and if I can answer it I will."

"Well I have seen Samson kiss you when he asked you to marry him. What is it like to be kissed? Do people still kiss when they're married? You both looked like you enjoyed kissing."

"Dear sweet Mary Beth and my own Alicia, kissing is wonderful. The man you love takes you in his arms and holds you against his body. You have seen animals in the barnyard, so you know males and females are made different. Have you ever touched a hand and felt sparks fly between you and the man who has your hand in his?"

We both said yes

"A kiss is for that special person. No one else." she admonished, "Love feelings flow all around you and life is in tune to nature and all is well with your soul. Your heart sings and the loved one touches you and you melt."

Mrs. Thomason kissed us both on the cheek. We heard the music start and the church woman came to get us.

"Alicia Thomason and Mary Beth Hamilton were part of the bridal party." A friend said after the day ended. It sounded so elegant said that way. But I'm ahead of myself. Good thing you are only a book or else you would jump up and down with impatience.

The old church was grand. We enjoyed the long walk down the aisle behind Mrs. Thomason.

The candles were lit, and the flowers just right. I think Alicia and I saw Samson about the same time her mother did. All was well. The preacher went through the traditional ceremony.

But when he asked if anyone had any objection to the wedding, we saw the merchant from the umbrella stall and several others jump up and start talking at once.

The preacher held up his hand for silence and waited until it was quiet. He asked the merchant, "What is your reason for this outburst?"

The stall vendor said, "Most of us have known this woman by sight and from doing business with her over many years. She has always been a respectable person. He has bewitched her. She would never marry the Devil himself if she knew who he is and what he has done. I saw with my own eyes demons come up out of the ground and kill two men in front of me. Others here know about him, too."

Old preacher Potter said, "I watched him call out demons to heal a dead man. Those demons did as he said. Even if this woman wants to wrap herself up with the likes of him, there is her daughter to consider. Will she find herself under the roof of the devil, doing his bidding?"

I moved forward and said, "This man is good and kind. You know nothing if you believe what has been said. Merchant, why didn't you come to help me when a big brute of a man grabbed me right in front of you? You would have let him take me, wouldn't you? Why would you see evil instead of good when help arrived?"

I took a big breath and started again. "Preacher Potter don't you read in the Bible about Jesus raising people from the dead? And he told the disciples they could do even more than he had while he was here? You must be a false preacher if you only see evil and not the goodness of God."

I continued, "That's directly from the Bible. Preacher if you just quote the word of God as someone else told it, you don't have enough of God's word to be preaching, we must study the word daily before we can tell others."

Preacher Ames, from this church, said, "Amen. You have heard it out of the mouth of babes. Now, I want all of you to be seated and I'll continue this wedding, if you object to that you should leave right now." He waited about five minutes. Several left.

Alicia had her arms around her mother and Samson. I moved over into the big hug too. Samson looked right into Mrs. Thomason's eyes, and said, "After all this commotion I wouldn't blame you if you wanted to call off the wedding."

"Samson, I love you and I know none of those things are true. We are doing this until death do us part. Nothing else can separate us. Let us proceed with our wedding."

We enjoyed the rest of the ceremony as if nothing had happened. A nice reception was put on by the church ladies. It was a happy day. Alicia and I, and her mother, changed back into our regular clothes. Alicia was going home with me and Barney since Samson was taking her mother, his new bride, to the ocean for a whole week for their honeymoon.

After supper father asked me to come to his study. That was not a good omen. I saw immediately he was mad. His face had turned red. "Mary Beth, how do you keep getting into trouble? Do you want to scandalize our name? Do you do these things to thwart me? Why are you such an unruly child?"

"I don't know. I don't try to be bad. Am I bad? What have I done this time?" I didn't know what I had done.

"What have you done? I'm sure you know what you did at the wedding today. How could you? Acted as if you know more about the Bible than our preacher. You spoke out in Church. Women are not to speak in church, and against our preacher. Telling him, he didn't know what he was talking about, and that he should read the Bible himself and not let someone else tell him what to believe. What were you thinking? What got into you? Are you demon possessed? I do not know how I can make it up to Preacher Potter. We will be lucky if the whole family is not banished from our church. A disruptive child reflects badly on the parents. What do you have to say for yourself, young lady?"

"Father, my good friend was being attacked. Called the devil for helping Etta, Barney, and me, that day the men who wanted revenge on you died. When I spoke up everyone was surprised and started to listen to some sense about the merchant, the one who would have let them take me. He didn't do a thing to help us. He didn't even go for the constable."

I had to take a breath, and then continued. "Preacher Potter jumped in and called a godly healing of a dead man the work of the devil instead of seeing the truth that God is the one who heals. That's in the Bible, I have read it. Why didn't our preacher know that? If he is not studying the Bible, how can we trust what he tells us? Especially when we see him branding a good man as the devil. His judgment is in error. Perhaps the best thing for this family would be for that church to throw us out of their congregation. I…"

"That will be quite enough little lady! Go to your room right now!" He fairly screamed at me. I stormed up the stairs determined not to cry. How can one's own family misunderstand your motives and turn on you so badly? Of course, he and mother never pay much attention to us unless we are in trouble. Then the question is not what we did, but how it affects their standing in the community. If the church did remove our membership, I would see it as a good thing. Mother and Father would be devastated, wondering how they could ever hold their head up around town and in society. It might have far reaching effects on father's business dealings. I wonder sometimes if that's their reason for attending church at all. Do they go to worship God or to be seen by other important people?

Chapter 13

" *D*ear Diary,
    I have read the things I wrote down last time. I guess that was about two years ago. There is more to say on the church issue. The flock didn't expel us. But many repercussions came from my words about old preacher Potter. The board members decided he should have a nice retirement cottage and a small pension, so the new preacher could live in the house next to the church. Preacher Potter was not at all happy. He blamed me and told everyone in earshot about the wrong I did to him. He also spread the rumors that I was a witch. Me, Mary Beth Hamilton, a witch!

Samson told me about four months later, "Old Potter has a bad spot in him. Like an apple. It may have started out as a small bruise and gotten bigger with time. There is an old saying that one rotten apple can spoil the whole bushel. I think that is what happened to Potter. I feel sorry for him. I pray for him too that he will learn what is right and will change."

"Did you know, Mary Beth, that you hit his problem right on the nail? He couldn't read. So, all he said was what others told him. Our preacher Ames saw the man's face when you were speaking of that. He went to Potter and offered to teach him to read. They are becoming friends and the reading is moving along well. He also found out that Potter wasn't sure how long he could keep preaching. His knees and shoulders were giving him fits with pain. He was afraid to tell anyone about the pain. You made it possible for him to retire and have a small pension. I am proud of you for speaking out for me on our wedding day. You helped us see that it was our wedding day, our life, our special time and no one could put a damper on it."

Many other things have happened during the time I haven't written in this book.

Barnabas has graduated with Honors. Father is insisting he go to France for College. He doesn't want to go. I think he is in love with Alicia. He wouldn't tell me yes or no, when I asked. If he is father will be a problem.

I'm tired and will go to sleep now. Why does growing up have to be so hard? Good night little book.

Chapter 14

"Dear Faithful Diary,
You sit here waiting for me to open your pages and pour out my life.

Another couple of years have passed. I have had a proposal of marriage. I couldn't believe it when I heard about it. Father even thought it was a good match for me. I'm still fuming. This man is a wealthy landowner. In fact, he owns several farms and has families take care of them for him, like we do. The people get a place to live and some of the crops to use for themselves. At one time I remember father calling him an autocrat. When I said, "Father how could you possibly think he is a good match for me when I have heard you call him a tyrant. Do you care so little for me that you would marry me off to such a man?"

I started to cry. Not from what I had said but

from anger that he would even think of marrying me to an old man. Come to think of it, I think one of the first things I put into this book was that a man a little older might be nice. But I didn't mean ancient. I hardly ever cry so I learned something that day. With father, crying makes him give in to me. I will have to explore this tactic in other areas of life and test to see what works.

I didn't have to meet old Jonathan Charles Smythe. Father turned him down for me.

They are insisting I be part of the coming out parties in London this year, hoping I will find a suitable husband. Of the Ton members I have met through all these years there is no one who I have the least desire to meet again. Maybe someone who I haven't met or has been abroad for years could pique my interest. Is something wrong with me that I don't find men more appealing? Many, of my friends are already married. Being an attractive young woman is hard work.

The dressmaker has been here and measured every inch of me for the many new gowns she is making. To get ready for this ordeal is a chore; fittings all the time. Of utmost importance, never make the dressmaker mad. Last year one of my acquaintances Marla Lawton upset her dresser and when she arrived at the ball and her cloak was removed, the buttons down the front started popping off, everyone gasped. She was totally embarrassed.

I have no worries about anything like that. Alicia's mother, Mrs. Roberts now, is making all my clothes for this special round of parties and showing off.

They are really trying to marry me to a wealthy man. Father says, "Mary Beth, you need someone as rich as we are so you can be happy. You have been so privileged you would never be happy with less."

He may be right, but I hope I would take whatever comes and make the most of it. I really want romance, a once in a lifetime love, a forever man. Strong enough to temper my strong will and outspokenness, but gentle enough to let me be who I am inside. I want it all. A warm loving family so we can hug and kiss each other and be joyously happy.

Mother, Mrs. Roberts, Alicia and I got to go to the big city of London to shop. We visited many of the best Shoppes. In one place, the clerk asked if we would like to purchase several of those Thomason Button Pockets, to use in our new fashions. We went outside and laughed and laughed. Mother didn't understand why that was so funny. It looked like a good idea to her. We let her in on the fact that Mrs. Roberts had invented them when she was still Mrs. Thomason and sold the design and now everyone was using them, even the most exclusive seamstresses. Mother decided it was funny and laughed with us. That was the difference between Mother and Mrs. Roberts.

Mother had to decide if something was funny or if she could hug her children. Mrs. Roberts saw the fun and hugged and laughed first. I saw then that she was richer than my mother, in all the ways that count; love, joy and happiness. I know Barney and I have been hugged more by Mrs. Roberts than we ever were by our own mother. I do think Mother loves us but is not able to demonstrate it.

I want my man and children to have a wife and mother who can laugh, hug and kiss them. And make a real family life for us. I pray God will bring the right husband for me."

Chapter 15

Isaac smiled when he saw the next entry.

"Hello Friend Diary,

A whirlwind of weeks have gone by since I last entered anything. We leave for London in the morning.

It will be awhile before I write in you next time. I just wanted to jot down some of the things that have been going on with us.

I wanted Alicia to go to the balls and everything with me, but was told that was impossible, since she is not in the social class of the Ton. Mother finally suggested she could go as a companion and we could walk in the park together or visit the museums during the day. Mother would need to sleep most of the day, but if I didn't need that much sleep, we could see some of the town. My official chaperone would have to accompany us and be close at hand at all times.

Alicia was happy to have that small part in my great display to the world of high society. We found several of my gowns that would be good for her to wear around the big town as we saw the sights. They would have been good for me to wear to town but a whole wardrobe had been made for this outing.

You would have to be rich to take the kind of trip we are embarking on. Overwhelming amounts of luggage. Six carriages will be in our caravan to carry the baggage, food and servants and family. Mother, Alicia and I had a great number of bags for all the clothes, plus all the servants' needs.

We are staying two months. I should have met half the world by then. Father will come up the last week we are there. He will be looking to see if anyone is paying attention to me, then check them out to see if they fit his idea of my husband. After last time, I don't think I can put much faith in his choice. I will have to be diligent and see what I approve of for me.

Goodbye, for now, Dear Diary. I will write again when we return from my grand adventure.

Chapter 16

" **D**ear Diary,
　　　　Two months have flown past. I should have taken you with me. So many busy days. Where to start?

We arrived in London, near mid-day, exhausted and too hot. Luckily our London house that had been opened for the Season, was built of cool stone. What a relief. Our arms were tired from using our hand-held fans during the trip. Mother had several of the servants make up all the beds first thing. The kitchen help put the food away and the boxes inside the kitchen door. When they finished cook had a light meal ready. After they ate Mother sent them all to bed. If the servants awoke before us, they could start supper or wait until we were up too.

Father would have had a fit if he knew she had told the servants to take a nap. He would have ordered them to start the regular work right after we arrived. I noticed the grateful looks on the tired people's faces. Mother had made a tactical move and her people would trust her and be more loyal than ever. I guess I really hadn't paid much attention to how she ran the household. Now I started to watch how she did things. Many times, good servants are lost on trips like ours to houses that would treat them better.

If I did find a husband, I'd need to know how to run a household. I started asking Mother questions on how she did this or that. She was pleased that I asked her. I thought she was standoffish, maybe I needed to value her more as someone to learn from.

Mother was a good manager and showed me her lists of foods and clothes that were needed for this trip.

We went to bed early that night and were ready to start refreshed the next morning. Mother and I had several calls to make leaving our calling cards, and meeting friends who were home. When we arrived back at the cool house, we saw we had missed a few visitors who had left their cards for us. Another thing I learned about Mother is that she remembers names and is her own social secretary. If I am ever in that position, I'll need to hire someone to keep track of names, dates, places, and times. I always thought Mother just sat around the house all day. I never saw all the little behind the scenes problems that occurred and had to be handled. During our London outing with all the entertaining and being entertained, I saw how the hostess had to manage the invited guests. She had to invite certain people so they wouldn't be offended. Then she had to make sure she didn't seat someone who was feuding with another next to each other. Also care had to be taken to put shy people next to a conversationalist. The protocol for parties was amazing. It was like a board game. You move your pawn but only in the correct direction for it. There were consequences for not following the rules.

The Debutant High Tea that was held so all the debs could meet each other was fun. It was held at a big hotel, The Carlton del Mar. I thought this was funny, because it was not near the sea, but it sounds so nice and elegant. The dining room was set up for us, six per table, with the waiters dressed in formal black pants with white shirts, gloves and an immaculate white towel folded over one arm. The hostess moved the place cards with our names beautifully written in calligraphy to a different table following her chart plan. Each person moved to the next table and spent thirty minutes talking with that new group. This was a nice way to meet each of the debutantes and learn a little about each of them. We would be together at many gatherings during the next two months.

The tea was our first meeting for many of us. We had known many who were attending this event for years. It's funny, you look at a new person and instantly like or dislike them. What is that about? Some you disliked at first, can become friends. But most of the first impressions are how you always see them. Is it clothes, attitude, or just an inner instinct that makes that happen?

Mother was keeping me on track with my social

obligations. A few days after the tea, Mother surprised us by taking Alicia, our chaperon Mrs. Brooker, and I to the Carlton for dinner. We had been out shopping and were delighted to visit the Carlton. I couldn't believe Mother, being spontaneous. I was getting to like her more and more. Maybe she was realizing I was no longer that child she couldn't talk to but was growing into a young woman with interesting ideas to share.

At a table about two over from us was a young man who looked delicious. He looked my way with his steady solid blue eyes. I noted that they weren't the usual washed out blue. I loved his blue-black hair. I liked everything about him. He handed the waiter his menu and I saw the long fingers. He smiled as our eyes met and he made a slight wave.

Mother caught me as I was ready to wave and quickly slapped my hand. "What do you think you are doing? Young ladies don't wave at anyone. Is that a man? If so, he is out of my sight line and it is not permitted that I turn to inspect him. I thought we taught you better than that."

The food arrived and Mother's mood changed. She became the perfect happy hostess again. We went to a couple of other Shoppes after we left the Carlton. We declared it a perfect day.

Another free leisure day the four of us went to the famous Montclair Fountains and Gardens. Mother wrote on her note paper several names off their signs. "Our gardens are beautiful like these. I wonder if I could get plant name signs made? They would have to be strong enough to withstand the weather. I would prefer calligraphy, it is so lovely, but it might be hard to read down low like that. Maybe we could put them on stands that would be easy to read."

Alicia spoke up. "I think Samson could make them for you. Maybe he could make a pretty scroll. Mrs. Hamilton, put a little drawing with the flower names on your paper so you can show him what you want."

"Thank you, Alicia, that is a good idea." Mother said.

I looked up and saw that man again, just a few feet away. He caught my eye and waved that slight hand movement. I didn't try that again, just smiled. Mother came to stand beside me. He was gone. The feelings he stirred up in my body were so new and exhilarating. Shortly after that outing I started thinking about, my dark-haired man. It seemed each time we were out we saw him. He was probably a tourist trying to see all the sites in the guidebook, as we were doing.

Before the first ball, there were several parties. These were fun. But I saw no one who compared with the man I first saw at The Carlton. After the first ball Mother started sleeping in mornings, so Alicia and I went out with Mrs. Brooker. We went to the Fenton Art Gallery one day. I told Alicia, "I love that painting of the roses in the red lacquer vase."

Alicia stood pointing at the picture behind me. "Mary Beth, look at that painting; at him."

I turned and walked over to stand in front of it. "Oh, my goodness, it does look like the man we have been seeing around town."

Mrs. Brooker looked closely, then stated in her droll voice, "I'm sorry to discourage you but it couldn't be anyone we have seen. See the painter's name? He is very famous and died many years ago."

Alicia said, "Maybe so, but that is the man we have seen, or someone who looks like him." We saw him again at an outdoor market while we were buying fresh flowers. I got a little wave and a big luscious smile. Someone walked by and when they passed, he was gone.

The second ball came and went. It was great fun but now I was spoiled. My black-haired man wasn't there. I wondered if there was any way I could meet the man that was so attractive to me. He invades my daydreams and night dreams. I didn't even know if he was attracted to me. He smiled and waved but that was all. He had never tried to meet me. How sad it makes me to think we will be going home soon, and I have not met my man. He could be married already. That thought made me sadder still. None of it mattered if I didn't meet him. I decided I would say something to him next time I saw him. I'd introduce myself.

This wouldn't be proper but how else was I going to find out who he is and what he sounds like and if he would like to meet me? Women are supposed to let the man make the first move. Has life for women always been so hard?

The round of card parties and luncheons for the debs kept us busy from day one. Several of the girls were already spoken for right after the first Ball. Many more spoken for after the second Ball. I had interviews with several young men, but they were boring. I finally admitted to myself that I had my heart set on the man with the black hair and lovely blue eyes, whose name I didn't know. Mother was rather disappointed since several of those gentlemen were "very good catches" as the saying goes.

I was dressed in my third ball gown, a lovely white flowing concoction. My dark brown eyes sparkled, and my dark brown hair was up in a chignon, with white fluffy feathers that were artfully attached to it.

Everyone with me had told me how beautiful I looked. Staring into the large standing mirror. I felt beautiful. I was very excited. Something wonderful would happen that night, I just knew.

I danced and drank punch and danced and danced. The evening was slipping away, only two more dances. Then he was walking toward me, with punch in his hand. I reached for the amulet around my neck and mentally pleaded for help, to do just the right things so he would fall in love with me.

"I have paid off your two next dance partners so I can meet you and dance with you. First, I thought you might like some punch. May we sit over here?" he asked as he was moving to two chairs sitting a bit away from everyone else.

"This is fine, thank you." I sat down. He handed me the drink and sat beside me. Every nerve in my body tingled. I hadn't realized how parched I was after dancing all night. We sat quietly for a few minutes. How refreshing to drink the too sweet liquid and catch up on breathing. The music started for the waltz. He stood and held out his hand to me.

We walked to the dance floor and joined in the gay whirling.

"You dance very well, Miss Hamilton. You are very beautiful," he said.

"Thank you, sir. The waltz is my favorite dance. I'm sorry, you didn't introduce yourself therefore I don't know your name." *All I do know is that your blue eyes are more remarkable than I first thought.*

"Let me be mysterious. I will not tell you who I am. Perhaps I'm a rogue, a banker, or noble, or captain of a ship, maybe even a pirate," he teased.

We both laughed but I wanted to know his name. His voice was perfect to my ear. I wanted the dance to go on forever. When the music stopped, we found our same chairs.

"Why would you pay to dance with me?" I asked.

"When I heard you had told an old fire and brimstone preacher that he didn't know what he was talking about and he needed to read his Bible more, I had to meet you." He grinned.

"That was a long time ago now, are they talking about it here in London?"

"No. I heard about you many years ago. This is the first time I have had the opportunity to meet you. Every time I have seen you around town you were well chaperoned. I'm sorry you got scolded on my account when you started to wave back that first time. I was surprised your mother didn't look to see who was waving at her daughter, but decided she would think that was bad manners. Is that right?"

"Yes, that was the reason."

The music started. "This is the last dance of the

ball. Will you be so kind?" he asked, holding out his hand.

"Yes, kind sir. It will be my honor."

The music was wonderful, and the ballroom was magnificent, it was lighted well with many candles, and thousands of flowers scented the whole space. This gorgeous man was holding me tighter than was allowed. I didn't say a thing about it, just enjoyed his nearness. The dance ended and we promptly returned to our chairs and with a hand kiss and a bow, he was gone. My heart clenched. My dream man had entered my life and gone like a poof of smoke, without even telling me his name. Maybe if he had not held me in his arms, making me want to stay right there forever, it would have been easier to forget him. I didn't think I would ever forget him. How could he get such a hold on me in such a short time, without me knowing any more about him than his looks and my ardor for him? How can you have those kind of feelings for a stranger like you will die if you don't get to have him in your life. My forever man, that is what I want him to be.

When Mrs. Brooker and I arrived home, Father was waiting up. He called me into the salon. It was warm in there. He and Mother were playing cards. Since father arrived, Mother sent Mrs. Brooker to the ball with me.

Mother asked, "Did you have fun dear? You look absolutely beautiful."

"Yes, have you ever been in that ballroom? It was lighted with thousands of candles and the flowers were grand to see and smelled lovely, at first then later became a bit overwhelming. That room is wonderful. The musicians outdid anything I had heard before. Everyone whirling to the music was such a joyous sight to see." I twirled around a couple of times, for my parents to see how my dress flowed so lovely with the moves.

Father asked, "Have you met anyone you are the least bit attracted to? You have had several good suiters, well qualified. Did you meet anyone else tonight?"

"No, Father." I half lied. Well I hadn't been introduced to him. That implies you at least knew his name, I reasoned to myself. I was tired and wanted to dream about him. I excused myself and went up to bed.

Even better, Alicia was awake and wanted to hear everything that happened that night. I told her, not leaving out any of the details. We talked and laughed a long time. Then sleep came. Also, the dreams of a lifetime with my handsome stranger. Home, children, and portraits on the wall were included in this fantasy, with books, in a big library. I remembered the dream after I awoke and tried to think what my mind was wanting me to pull out of it. Something there I needed to know more about.

Alicia awoke quite a while after I did. We had stayed up very late, so she needed her sleep. I told her about my dream and that there was something there that I was trying to remember because there was something I needed to do.

Alicia was laughing when I got the dream told. "Didn't you hear what you said?"

"Maybe I'm dense but I missed whatever you heard."

"Mary Beth, get dressed. We have to go to the gallery where we saw his portrait!" Alicia said.

"Oh, my, I didn't remember the picture of him. Maybe the gallery people will know the name of the person in the painting."

Right after we ate breakfast with Mother and Father, we were off with Mrs. Brooker. We had to wait in the carriage a few minutes until the gallery opened. I asked to speak with the owner, Mr. Eldon. He was very nice, but not much help. He told us, "A man brought it in one day and paid me to hang it for one day only. I know nothing about the person who brought it in or who the man in the picture was supposed to be, however that artist died over eighty years ago and he was famous for his portraits. Wait a minute it seems that after he was gone and I looked at it hanging on the wall, I thought the man who brought it in looked like the man in the portrait and he would now be about the age of the painted gentleman, when the likeness was made. I'm sorry I don't know how you would find out any more about them." Mr. Eldon walked with us out of the gallery and said, "I wish you luck in discovering more about this mystery."

I waited until we were safely back in our room to say to Alicia, "He wanted us to see that painting. But how would he know we were going to the gallery? It was there when we came in that day. And it was only there one day. Now what do I do? I still don't know his name."

Alicia volunteered, "We could go walk in the park. Maybe he would find us. Now that he spoke to you last night, he might talk to us there."

A little after lunch, off we went by carriage fully chaperoned by Mrs. Brooker, to walk in the park. It was not long after we got there that we spotted him near the flower vendor's stall. He was only half turned toward us.

A dirty urchin started toward us. I put my hand on the amulet in my pocket and said, "Safety Now." As the child snatched my bag, I closed my parasol and hit him on the head, and he fell on the sidewalk. I pulled my reticule out of his grubby little hands. "You can wake up now and go," I said, hoping he wasn't dead like the man from my childhood. He started to run away and then turned back toward me and shouted, "You are a witch!"

That's all I needed. I looked for my man hoping he hadn't seen the little incident. He was closer and smiling right at me. He had witnessed everything.

He came over and tipped his hat to us. "Good day ladies. I moved close because I thought I was going to be able to help a damsel in distress, but she took care of herself. Might I be able to walk with you through the park?" He had addressed this to Mrs. Brooker. I have no idea why, but she said, "If the young ladies don't mind then we shall walk together."

We nodded our approval. The walkway was very wide, but we fell into step, my man and I in front and Alicia and Mrs. Brooker behind us. We stopped often to look at certain plantings. This man knew a lot about different flowers. When we stopped, we all gathered for easier talking It was lively and fun. When we started to tire, he suggested the outdoor café just at the end of the walk we were on now.

That was agreeable. He ordered a mini-tea. The waitress brought fresh tea, crumpets, nuts and cucumber finger sandwiches with a fancy cookie for each of us.

"I love this tea. Oh, I would like to have this cookie recipe," Alicia said.

"Me too," I said.

Our benefactor for the day looked at us and smiled. "Don't tell me you both cook? You're too young and beautiful for cooking in a hot kitchen."

"We both cook very well. Ruthie our cook and Mrs. Roberts, Alicia's mother have taught us well."

He looked closely at me and said, "Let me get this straight, you cook, you protect yourself and you tell off old fire and brimstone preachers?"

Alicia said, "You saw her ward off that little thief. You should have seen her tell the old preacher. That happened at my mother's wedding. He and some others were trying to stop the marriage. They were saying bad things about Samson, the man marrying my mother. He called Samson the Devil himself.

Mary Beth jumped up and pounded a book on the pew for attention and gave everyone a big, big shock. Women still aren't permitted to speak in church. She lit into that old preacher and really made people think about what she had said. The disruption was over, and they left. We continued with the ceremony. A couple of months later my new stepfather Samson told Mary Beth that what she had told the preacher was right and he couldn't read. His congregation pensioned him and gave him a house to live out his life. Our preacher saw the man's face when she hit his problem right on the nail. He went to him and has taught him to read.

When Mary Beth found out, we made cookies and took him some peach jam we had made and a Book of Psalms he could put into his pocket. She gave these to him and apologized for her treatment of him. He accepted the apology but we're not sure he still doesn't think she is a witch. Now all that is left is for you to try Mary Beth's cooking."

We were all laughing.

The dark-haired man said, "I would like to try your cooking." More laughter. "It amazes me you are in the right and tell off the old guy and still go and apologize to him."

I said, "I was in the right defending my friend. But it was wrong to expose his secret. It worked out well by the church getting a new pastor and giving him an income and a place to live. The old man was having a lot of pain and didn't know what he would do if he had to stop preaching. He could have been left penniless, with no job and no home."

We enjoyed a leisurely stroll around the other path that brought us back where we started our walk.

When we got there I said, "You still haven't told us your name. It is only polite that you do so. We have been delighted by our time with you today. Please tell us."

"I will tell you when the time is right. Not before then. Thank you, ladies for the nice stroll in the park."

With that he turned and walked away.

The carriage driver saw our exchange with the dark-haired man. I hoped he wouldn't mention it to anyone. Mother wanted to hear all about our day. We told her about the flowers and the lovely weather for a stroll and the mini tea. We told her how we laughed and really enjoyed the outing. No one mentioned the wonderful man who shared it with us. I wondered how bad is the sin of omission? I'm not a secretive person. Yet here I was half lying and leaving out important parts of what I tell my parents.

Several other suitors had shown up, only to impress me with how much I was missing my man. We hadn't seen him after the walk in the park. I thought if I didn't see him soon, I would pine away the rest of my life. I'm not usually that dramatic either. But pining is what it felt like.

Our trip home to Amber Manor was long and tiring. Mother again had a cold dinner prepared and sent the servants to bed early. The next day the house buzzed with activities; cooking and cleaning. I caught Mother humming a tune. We smiled and went about what we were doing. That felt nice."

Chapter 17

S arah pored Isaac another cup of coffee. He took a long drink before he began again

"Dear Diary,

It has been a long time since I picked you up. I reread the last entry. I'm still pining. But not wasting away as I have heard goes along with pining. Still no word from my man. He is not mine, but I wish he was mine. I still dream about him.

Several nice fellows have been here to visit with father and the family. When the first one arrived, I went to father to have a talk. He didn't like what I said but he finally agreed. "Father, I don't want to marry now. I'm waiting for the man that's right for me. When he shows up, I'll tell you. Please don't make any agreements or arrangements with anyone until I let you know it's my man."

"That's what fathers do; they choose the man for

their girls. You see I must know he can take care of you and that he will be good to you. That his finances are in order."

"Father, how would Mother fare if anything happened to you? Will she be able to keep the house and servants and have everything go on as it is?" I asked.

"What an impertinent question." He bellowed. "You have no need to know about my business."

"Father, women do need to know about these things. Does Mother have any idea that she will be provided for if you died? How many of your friends over the last several years have been left impoverished when they lost their husbands? I know of at least four. Mrs. Parsons, Mrs. Jones, Mrs. Lambeth and Mrs. Arlington, all have lost their homes to creditors. None of them were prepared for work and had to depend on other family members to take them into their homes. What do you think that would do to a woman who is used to the command of a big mansion? She has skills but she can't use them. Because of her name or title, she can't go to work for someone else as a housekeeper. I do believe some of them might have changed their names and done just that, become housekeeper for a rich family. But how humiliating if one of her old friends found out. People are not as kind to widows as they should be." I went over and hugged him. "Don't you see what I'm telling you. When Alicia's father died her mother was a good seamstress and knew about herbs and pretty plants to sell. She cooked for a couple of people too. They got by well because of her skill and knowledge," I said.

"But she is lower class, so she was taught those things. Women like your mother are trained to care for their homes. She was trained well. I have never had the servant problems most households run into," Father said.

"Have you told Mother that you're proud of the way she takes care of your home?"

"I'm sure she knows I am," Father answered.

"Do you love her?" I asked.

"We have been married a long time," he said.

"That's not what I asked you," I said.

"This is quite enough, go to your room, young lady. I'll not have you questioning me and speaking of such things, you should be ashamed of such talk." Father fumed.

I saw his face getting redder and redder as he said this last. I hugged him again "I'll go but please think over what I have said. It's important.

Dear Diary,

Mother and Father were frantic. I have refused to go to the Debutant Balls and surrounding parties and have a season this year. I told them, "Last year didn't take, I found no one for me. There is no reason to go back this year and see the same old suitors again. Putting myself on display for another season would be a waste of money." I have refused the dressmakers and all the attendant rush to follow the social circle. They were very disappointed in me.

They're worried their friends and colleagues would look down on them for not giving me a second season. Maybe they would think they didn't have the money to spend. Or worse, that they did have the money but were too tight to do it. Several young girls went through this ordeal three or four outings before getting a husband. Some girls I know would do anything not to become an old maid.

I haven't dared to voice this to my parents, but I have decided my man is the only one for me. If I cannot have him, then I'll be a spinster. This is not an unpleasant idea to me. I can always find something interesting to do. Solitude is fine with me. When you want apple pie, why settle for an apple. I love apples but I like apple pie more. Who says all there is in life for a woman is marriage and children? Well, to answer that question, I guess the answer is MEN!

Someday if I change my mind and want to marry someone other than the man I want now, I am sure there will be many around.

Dear Diary,

It's about six months since I wrote last. The season is over. Father was surprised that several of the suitors that remembered me from last year have come to call. Not my man, however. It has been a lot of entertainment that has come to naught. Father thinks I should take one of this batch. But, NO!

Chapter 18

" *D*ear Diary,

Barnabas, as we are only allowed to call him now that he has graduated Cum Laud from that elite school in France, is home again. Alicia and I stood on the porch at her home when his carriage pulled up. He jumped out as soon as it stopped. He grabbed Alicia off her feet and twirled her around. They were laughing. "Oh, my love, I could hardly wait to get back to you!"

I know Alicia was talking to Barnabas, but I didn't hear her words. I just know that's how it would be if my handsome black-haired man with the just right blue colored eyes, came home to me. Nothing around us would matter. I would want to kiss him forever.

Finally, they stopped kissing and acknowledged my presence, and enclosed me in their hug. Mrs.

Roberts came out on the porch and joined in the group hug. She had us come inside and eat a small meal she prepared. Samson hugged Barnabas too, and said, "It's good to have you home son."

Barnabas and I had to go and face our parents. "Mary Beth, you can't tell Mother and father that we stopped by Alicia's house first. Father is going to hit the roof when he hears I still want to marry her. You heard the row before I finally went to college. I only went because Alicia told me she would wait for me to return to her. As you know we have been writing constantly. That's how I got through it. I didn't come home on breaks but signed up for extra classes so I could finish as quickly as possible. There is a certification test in the place I desire to set up my practice to be done and then I'll have a license to practice medicine."

"Doctor Barnabas Hamilton, what a nice name for a medical man. I'm so proud of you, brother, graduating with honors. That's great. Oh look!" I cried as the house came into sight and the amber glow colored the gray rocks so wonderfully.

"That's a sight I have missed in my time away from all of you. The amber glow on the walls is so special," Barnabas said.

"What are you saying? You didn't miss me? I shall be heartbroken unless you take that back," I said.

He hugged me. "You know I missed you. Alicia told you I asked about you often, Mary Beth. What about the man you met last year? No word at all? Alicia said you were pining away and may become a spinster, an old maid. But you look mighty good for a woman pining for her lost love."

"That shows what you know about lost loves. Your love for Alicia is solid and she will be your always love forever. I'm happy for you both, by the way. I don't even know my man's name. How does one fall in love with a man who didn't even trust her with his name? He could be a thief, pirate or anything, even married for all I know. If I knew where he was, I would go to him and plead for him to marry me."

The carriage rolled up to the front steps. Barnabas handed me out. We went up the steps to greet Mother and Father. Barnabas hugged them both. I took the opportunity to do the same. We all sat in the large salon with light blue walls and gold gilt chairs with blue velvet seats Barnabas answered questions about life at school.

The big blow up came after dinner tonight while we were sitting in the salon. Barnabas announced, "Father, Mother and Mary Beth, Alicia and I would like to invite you to our wedding on Sunday after church. A small reception will follow the ceremony."

Mother put her hand to her heart and declared, "Why would you give your mother such short notice? How will I ever get a new dress made in time? Can't you wait a bit until I'm prepared? Why did you wait so long to tell us?" She looked worried.

"I forbid it! You can't marry that girl. I told you before you went to college that she is not of our class and would never be good enough to marry you. We would never be able to raise our heads in this community again. Have you lost your senses? As a doctor you will need a woman of good background and a big dowry to help you get yourself established." Father shouted.

"Mother to answer your question on why you got a late invitation, after all the arrangements were made, what father just said is what I knew his reaction to my marriage to Alicia would be. I'm marrying her with or without your blessings and whether you attend or not. I hope you will all be there. We will leave for France right after the reception. I already have a partnership in a four-man doctor's group. We will rotate days when each man works so we can get some time with our families. Our small house is already leased and ready for us to move into. Good night." He left the room.

Barnabas had only been home, a few hours and now he was getting married on Sunday. Father ranted and raved for what seemed like hours.

I said. "Father if you don't attend like you said, how could you raise up your head up in society again? A quick wedding will bring gossip and all kinds of problems with your friends. You must attend Barnabas, your only son's wedding, or it will be even worse. The gossip will be…problems in that family. He hurt his parents by disobeying their council. The girl must be with child. Maybe the girl had something bad she knew and forced him to marry her. These are just some of the accusations I have heard in similar situations."

Father said, "Mary Beth, how can you of all people defend him? He has lost his mind. You should help him stop this nonsense. You have caused us grief by not even looking for an eligible man, and he has disgraced us by choosing a totally unsuitable woman."

I said, "He has not lost his mind. He has lost his heart and that occurred many years ago. Be happy for him. He did as you insisted by going to France and he has finished his doctor's degree. He would have run away that night years ago when you had that last big confrontation. Barnabas was ready to take Alicia and leave you here never to return. Alicia talked him out of that plan, by telling him she would wait for him no matter how long. She didn't want Barnabas to make a rift between you, by him choosing her over you. He has what he needs for the best life he can have, with Alicia. You have known her for a long time too. She loves him with all her heart, and he loves her. They have waited a long time for this marriage. Don't you want the best for Barnabas?"

I started out the door then turned and said, "I'm attending my brother and my best friend Alicia's wedding. Decide what you want to do. It will of course affect your future grandchildren if you decide not to be there. Good night, Mother, Father."

Mother said, "But how will we get dresses made?"

"We will wear ones we already have in our wardrobe. I'm sure you have something that will be suitable. You will look beautiful as you always do, Mother."

I hadn't realized until we went to my coming out parties that Mother needed a great deal of compliments over her looks. A beautiful woman that was not very sure of herself was hard for me to understand. I had always been a confident person. When I saw her need, I started giving the compliments and had even told father he should tell her every time they went out how nice she looked. I don't know if he did or not.

Our house was abuzz. Ruthie, the cook, went down to the church and talked with the ladies giving the reception. We added to the reception food and provided lots of flowers, and rolls of lace for the ribbons and big bows for the center aisle pews.

I instructed Mother to answer snooty questions, when asked, about how Barnabas could marry below his station in life by saying "We are so glad that he has found a wonderful woman who will love him and cherish him all her life. We have known Alicia and her family for years. We want him to be settled and we know Alicia will make him happy. We moved the wedding time up because Barnabas is in a doctor's group and needs to return to France right away."

Mother went around the house repeating it many times during the days that followed. I noticed she hummed again. That always makes me smile, to know that she does really have music in her soul.

Sunday after church service, the wedding began. Mother and Father were seated by the ushers. Mother was wearing the surprise dress made for her by Alicia's mother from some material we had all liked on the shopping trip we had all taken to create my coming out clothes. The light blue with darker blue design was perfect for her hair and complexion. I told Mother how lovely she looked in it. Father saw her coming toward him and took her hand and said, "You're as beautiful now as when I married you all those years ago."

Stunned she said, "Why, thank you kind sir."

Barnabas stood beside preacher Ames. Samson walked the aisle with Alicia. She looked magnificent. The layered tulle dress was a sight to behold, and the young woman in it was perfection. The vows were given, and the couple married. The reception went off with no snide remarks or problems. The wedding was a great success. All too soon the happy couple had departed for their trip to France. A new and exciting life awaited them. Doctor Barnabas Hamilton and his wife Alicia Thomason Hamilton.

Even Father mentioned, "Glad we attended. They look so joyous together. I gave them my blessings and some money before they left us."

Chapter 19

At this point Alicia raised her hand and her grandson stopped reading the diaries. Alicia said, "I'm sorry, but I need to rest. Would you mind if we continue to read tomorrow?"

We all agreed and were entering the hallway when the front door burst open and a young disheveled crazy woman ran up to Eva. "You killed him!" she shouted. "He wanted to marry me, so you killed him! It was supposed to be you that died, not William! You're a witch for sure. William told me about your evil talisman made by witchcraft that had spells put on it. He hid it. You must be very strong in your witchery to kill him without it!"

The butler and Katherine arrived about the same time, having heard everything. He caught the girl's hand just as she was reared back to hit Eva, who was clutching the Amulet of Safety at her waist, through her clothes.

"Safety now," Eva said.

The young woman, started to howl like an injured animal, then she fainted.

At least Eva hoped she just fainted. *So, my old childhood friend Pearl Garver knew about William's plan to kill me. What am I going to do? If I have her arrested as an accomplice, everything will come out. How embarrassing to have a husband who wanted you dead. The poor girl thought he would marry her when I was out of the way. I really believe Pearl has been badly used and would have been tossed aside as soon as he got his hands on my money. He would have been looking for someone with more money. I wonder if he had already* chosen *a replacement for me. If I let her go, she might try to kill me herself. She is out of her mind with his loss. If we send her to a madhouse that would be awful. I have heard they have terrible conditions there. How sad that one man can make one woman crazy and the other his would-be victim. Was William deranged too? Dear God, I need to know how to handle this problem. Strangers have heard what Pearl said. Alicia hinted that she knew the real story of William's death was something like this earlier in the day.*

Sarah said to the butler, "Donald, please take Miss Garver to one of the unused servant's rooms and lock her in for the night, have someone stand guard. Please ask Doctor Webb to attend to her. Don't tell the others what happened. Say, 'she has been overwrought, and Mrs. Smythe said to watch to make sure that she is protected'."

"Yes, Madam," He picked up the frail girl and checked to see that she was breathing. She was and he moved off down the hall with her in his arms.

Alicia said, "Eva, I'm so glad to see you have the amulet with you. Your grandmother was afraid that after the big scare was over you would take it off thinking it had done the job and was no longer needed. I saw you thinking 'I hope she has only fainted,' as clear as if you had spoken it. You were right to worry about that. The two men who meant to harm young Mary Beth were really dead."

How they got any sleep that night Eva would never know. Maybe sleep takes us because we have no other direction to go right then. Maybe it's a place where we go to get away from all the evils in our world. Perhaps God provides that rest to work out what the next move will be.

After breakfast Eva asked the doctor to come to her father's office with her. The room still smelled like Father's fine tobacco. Very seldom was anyone in there, it was usually closed off to keep the heat in the rooms we used. It was very cool in here that morning. They sat in the big leather chairs placed across from each other beside the fireplace that Donald had prepared and lighted for their use.

"Doctor Webb, you saw a very disturbed woman, a Miss Pearl Garver, who came here last night. She was stopped before she could harm me. She has some very strange ideas and believes I tried to kill William. I don't know what to do about her. If I called the constable and had her put away, some unpleasant memories of mine would need to be told. If I let her go, she might try to attack me again. I believe she has gone crazy, but I hear those asylums are terrible places. I would hate to send her there. Will you see her again and let me know what you think I should do. I value your opinion. I'll wait for you here."

Doctor Webb said, "Don't fret yourself Eva. I have an idea. I'll go to Miss Garver now and see what can be done."

Eva paced the floor until he returned. She wore the carpet thinner. Father paced those same spaces when he was upset or worried. They had decided at breakfast that they would wait until after the mid-day meal to resume reading Grandmother Mary Beth's diaries. They had all morning to decide their next move in Miss Pearl Garver's future.

Doctor Webb knocked on the office door then entered when she called out. They sat in the chairs by the fire's warmth again.

"Eva, she acts like she has been drugged. She was passed out but breathing well, I didn't give her anything last night. It was hard to awaken her. When she did come around, she started her wild ranting. Says she wants to kill you like you killed her William. She also said it should have been you that died not William, that you're a true witch. Or you would have died, and he would have married her. It sounds as if he was having an affair with her. Did you know about that?"

"Doctor Webb, promise you will tell no one what I tell you." He nodded. "Her cousin Jane Garver, my good friend, told me awhile back, of her cousin's disgraceful behavior with William. Pearl had told Jane that William was going to marry her soon. We thought he would divorce me, which would have been a scandal. We in our wildest dreams never thought he would try to kill me by pushing me off my horse as we were racing them full speed." I shuddered with the telling of it. "I haven't told anyone about what really happened."

"Eva girl, I thought as much when you got back to the house after the accident. When you were born, your grandmother told me, "Doctor, you will have to look after Eva here, she will need the Amulet of Safety." She had told me about it when she was waiting with your grandfather as he was dying. She was out of her head and frantic until I found it on the top of her dresser in a little velvet bag and handed it to her. She calmed right down and the problem she was having with a breathing difficulty stopped. She had looked like something grabbed her heart and wouldn't let any air into her lungs. I think that episode scared me more than it did her. What was the miraculous thing that happened that saved you?"

"I haven't told it because I thought people might think I had gone crazy. I would hate to have anyone know William tried to kill me. We had been having a lovely day with sunshine and happiness and all the while he was being good to me, he was plotting my demise. What Miss Pearl Garver said last night about William hiding the Amulet so I wouldn't have it for safety is right. William did hide it.

I accused my best friend Katherine of taking it in front of a maid, to see if any of the servants would give us a clue about what happened to it. When Katherine was sleeping Grandmother Mary Beth's ghost came to her and then me and led us down to the stable to an old can. The amulet was under some nails in the can. If my amber hadn't been protected by glass and the velvet bag it might have received damage. Grandmother insisted that no one know I had it back."

"Glad to know she is still protecting you," Doctor Webb said.

"I did what she said, and it saved me. I'll tell the rest in a minute. Would you like coffee? I had Katherine bring a pot before you got back."

"Yes, I'm a coffee drinker. And I do want to hear the rest of the story. I'm sorry you have had to go through so many bad things, Miss Eva," Doctor Webb said.

Eva noticed how warm the room had gotten now that the fire had been burning all morning. She asked if he would like to move a little farther from the fireplace?

"No dear at my age, the warmth helps the old bones."

She was glad of his answer. The telling about William had left her cold. She uncovered the coffee pot and poured hot coffee and gave them each a sweet roll. They ate and drank in silence. Once they had their fill, she put the dishes back onto the tray, and Eva finished the story.

Eva said, "The sun was bright, and we walked and talked, and I thought things were better than ever. We had been having some rough times. Especially after I confronted him about Miss Garver. He left for several weeks. William came back and acted good."

She continued. "He had been home only a short time. We were riding out every day taking a picnic basket and walking and riding always ending with us racing the long way back home. We raced full speed. William came up beside me, he pushed me off my horse. I was halfway over the side with no way of catching myself, I would die. Giant hands stopped my fall and lifted me around my waist and sat me back upright on the saddle. I saw Grandmother's ghost standing in the path in front of William. My horse was slightly turned away by the unknown hand, so she didn't see the ghost. While I was turned, William's horse saw the ghost. He whinnied and reared straight up, throwing William into the big tree. He hit with an awful thud. I knew he was dead."

Eva said "William's horse ran off as fast as he could go, my horse got scared. I walked Candy around and around until she was calm again. I sat beside this murderous person, my husband. I knew the frightened horse would go back to the stable, and the farmhands would search for us. It seemed like hours. I got colder by the minute, which was odd because it was a warm day. I thought about all the things that happened and was glad he was dead. And it wasn't me that died, with him getting away with it. I'm sure he would have had no problem telling everyone about how I fell from my horse and broke my neck. Leaving out the part about how he pushed me off. I was so mad that he tried to kill me. I screamed and screamed into the open air glad no one could hear me. I was thankful for divine intervention. I thanked God for his protection in such a miraculous way."

"How do you think the amulet worked in that instance?" Doctor Webb asked.

"I'm not sure how it works. I didn't say anything. And I didn't have time to try to hold it in my hand. I think having it on my person was all I needed. I never believed it was cursed as people thought. I think when it was created, Samson put blessings on it for protection. I think he might have had God's special sight and knew Mary Beth needed protection. Perhaps from what you told me, maybe she had such an insight when I was born that I would need protection too. These things happened so fast; I don't think William had a chance to know that he failed to kill me. I don't believe a demon would have protected me. From what I have read in the Bible, God protects, and the devil tries to steal, kill, and destroy. I believe those big hands of safety were of an angel. I don't understand why I couldn't talk to Grandmother. She spoke to us when she showed us the hidden amulet, after what happened with William, she disappeared. There was plenty of time, she could have spoken to me." Eva said.

A messenger came in and handed a note to the doctor. He thanked the man, read the note and said. "I have a solution for you. I wrote a nice widow I know, a Mrs. Lester. She needs work. I ask if she could take on a boarder, and that the girl would need to be watched like a hawk. I thought she might be off in the head. She should be locked in her room during the night but should be able to be out during the day. Mrs. Lester has written that it would be a godsend for her to care for Miss Garver. Her older son and daughter-in-law live close by and they told her they would help if the girl became a problem and the daughter at home has agreed to help also. She is a young widow, too. When her husband died in a fall at work, she came back to live with her mother. I don't think she will marry again.

Would you be willing to pay for Miss Garver's room and board or should we ask her relatives?" Doctor Webb asked.

"While this is a great solution to my problem, I don't feel inclined to pay to care for a woman who knew about William's evil plan to murder me, and she tried to perpetrate an attack on me herself. I'm sorry for Miss Garver. William used her badly and I'm sure as soon as he had my money, he wouldn't have married her as he promised. Would he have killed her so she couldn't tell about his plans to do away with me? I'm inclined to believe he would. I'm positive in my heart that he would have found he was in a better position with my money to marry a woman of higher social standard and matched wealth. The more wealth you have the better your prospects. I have wondered how many women he would have killed for their money, if he had lived and I was dead? Did he already have a successor to me picked out?" Eva said.

"Do you want me to approach Miss Garver's family, then?" the doctor asked.

"I want to go with you. I have known them a very long time. I'll explain that if they don't pay Mrs. Lester to care for her, privately, criminal charges will be brought against her and she could draw the death penalty. I'll try not to go into the details. But this must be dealt with quickly. Will you be ready after the noon meal doctor?" Eva asked.

"Yes, that will be fine," Doctor Webb answered.

"Good. I'll have two carriages readied. You and I in one, and a guard and Miss Garver in the other. I want to wash up before lunch. See you back in the dining hall. Thank you, Doctor Webb."

To the disappointment of all of them, Eva explained that she and Doctor Webb were having to take care of the problem of Miss Garver this afternoon,and that she wanted to postpone the reading of Grandmother's diaries until the next day.

Alicia said graciously, "Of course, she must be dealt with speedily. We all understand, and I commend you for going with the doctor to see justice is done."

Sarah said, "Thank you doctor for providing this plan. It seems so much better than placing a woman in prison. Especially one we have known for years. It is sad that she has become unbalanced and dangerous. I'm proud of you, Eva, for being so strong and goodhearted."

When she was taken to the carriage, Miss Garver began to rant as soon as she saw Eva.

The guard hurriedly put her into the second carriage. We were off on the chore to inform the Garver family of their daughter's criminal behavior. Eva hoped they would accept the information and send her off to Mrs. Lester. Doctor Webb would tell them it would be payment in advance each month so the kind widow would be able to purchase whatever was needed to care for their daughter. Eva told him it should be a very generous payment. He agreed. Mrs. Lester was going to have her hands full. Eva prayed God would make the work tolerable and good for the Lester family.

They arrived at the Garver's beautiful home. The telling would be the hard part. Eva dreaded it.

The doctor took her hand and said, "Eva everything will be alright. I'm sure this family will want to do the best thing for their girl. You're brave and you can do this with grace and good will."

They were invited into the parlor where the family soon gathered to greet them. Well wishes were exchanged.

Doctor Webb stated, "We are here today on grave business."

The mother said, "Has something happened to Pearl, our daughter?"

Eva said, "She is alive. However, some big decisions must be made regarding her future right now. She is in the second carriage we brought, under guard. Last night she tried to attack me."

"Eva," Mrs. Garver said, "surely you're mistaken. Why would she try to harm you?"

"Because she was in love with my husband, William. I'm sure he led her astray. In her mind, it's I that should have died that day and not William. She has said all kinds of terrible things. Doctor Webb has checked her and thinks he has a solution. I would rather not press criminal charges against Pearl. But if you don't take the doctor's advice, then I'll have her arrested and she could get the death penalty. Doctor Webb please tell them your plan."

Mrs. Garver jumped up. "Eva, how could you

say such awful things about Pearl?"

"Mrs. Garver they're true. That's why I said them. Several people witnessed the ordeal last night."

Doctor Webb said, "We came here to you with an alternate plan so Pearl wouldn't go to prison. We knew you would want the best for her. I know a widow, Mrs. Lester who is willing to take care of her. Her daughter who is a young widow is living with her, and her son and his wife live close. I have requested that she be allowed to roam during the day with constant supervision. Then be locked in her room every night. I'll ask Doctor Tinley who lives close and is the Lester family doctor to care for her medical needs. You must make arrangements with him for his monthly bill. Mrs. Lester will need a monthly payment in advance of this amount." He handed the paper to Mr. Garver, and continued talking. Also, you must provide her clothes and any other needs."

Mr. Garver said, "This amount is more than I pay to stay at a fancy resort hotel for a month."

"Sir, you have no idea what it will be like to have a screaming girl who is willful and vindictive staying with you. She is distraught. The need to watch someone is a constant drain on a person, it takes a toll on a body. It's a reasonable price for the service you will receive. Besides, you won't have to deal with her condition yourself. Mrs. Lester will have her hands full. I'm hoping Pearl will identify with the grief of the two widows she will be in contact with and may be healed of her own grief."

Mr. Garver said, "Are you telling us our girl is

insane?"

"Not right now, but on the verge of it. She can go either way at this point. I have hope that she can be restored with the proper care. I know Mrs. Lester will do all she can for her."

"We want to see her," said Pearl's father.

"Send this note to the guard in the carriage with her and he will escort her inside." Doctor Webb handed the note to the father.

We waited in silence while Pearl was brought into the house. Her parents were horrified by her appearance. Her eyes were glazed and dull. She saw Eva and was instantly animated and started to wail. "What is that murderess doing here? She killed my Bill. She was supposed to die, not him, she is a witch." She let out a blood curdling scream. Her father came and took her in his arms where she cried and cried. When she cried herself out, she went limp in his arms and he said to the guard, "Take her, she needs help." Her father sat down and gave the money for her care to the doctor and took the paper the doctor handed him with Mrs. Lester's address on it." You can visit her in a few weeks. I'll have Doctor Tinley let you know when to come."

Eva and Doctor Webb left. She didn't know when Mrs. Garver had started to cry, but she continued the rest of the time they were there. After they were gone, Eva asked, "Will Mrs. Garver get sick from crying too much?"

"She could. But most likely she will dry up soon and be able to live with her grief at this turn of events. If her mind is weak, she may go off the deep end like her daughter."

Mrs. Lester was just as the doctor described her; round, not fat, with a smiling face and her house smelled so good from yummy cooking scents. She welcomed them and was shocked at the amount of money Doctor Webb handed her. "You shouldn't tell how much Mr. Garver will send you each month for her care. You will earn every penny and think, 'it's not enough.' This will be hard work. To always be on guard will be a strain. The order to lock her in at night may seem cruel to you and your daughter. But believe me it's necessary. You must be able to get some sleep. I hope that she will get better. She has had a mind turn, since a person she loved has been killed in an accident falling off his horse. Being around two women who have a similar story of loss might help her heal her own grief. We stopped at Doctor Tinley's on our way and he saw the patient. He gave me these pills for her. One three times a day with her meals. This bottle of pills is for sleeping. Give her one at bedtime. He will check regularly. If you need him just send someone for him. Mr. Garver will pay Doctor Tinley directly. Do you have any questions?"

"Yes, do you believe I'm capable of caring for Miss Garver?"

"I have every confidence in you dear lady. I wouldn't have asked you if I thought it would be too big of a task for you. I'm glad your daughter is here with you and will help and that your son also agrees that he would do whatever is necessary. Are you ready to meet her now?"

"I was sure when I sent the note back that said we would do this care for Miss Garver, that I was able. I just wanted to make sure you felt you had chosen correctly. Yes, I'm ready to meet her."

Doctor said, "Miss Eva would you wait in the carriage and have the driver move it forward, so Miss Garver won't see you right now?"

"Certainly. Mrs. Lester, it has been my pleasure to have met you. I'll pray for you to have God's peace and strength. Goodbye."

She hugged me. "Nice to meet you too, Miss Eva. God gets me through every day. I welcome your prayers. Goodbye."

When Doctor Webb got back in the carriage and we were on our way home, he said, "The first meeting went well. No screaming. She told Mrs. Lester she was hungry and was that meat pie she smelled. They were sitting down to eat when I left. It's in God's hands now."

Mrs. Lester sent each of them a meat pie and a muffin. They didn't know how hungry they were until he opened the basket and handed her one of the pies wrapped in a pretty yellow napkin. They arrived home late and ate what Martha had left for them. Eva's bed felt heavenly. She slept in the next morning and didn't go down until the mid-day meal. Doctor Webb had told the story of their journey the day before and what they hoped would be a happy ending for Miss Garver.

Chapter 20

After lunch they were all anxious to resume Grandmother's Diaries. Doctor Webb asked if he could join them. Eva told him since he knew so much of the stories of their lives it would be fine with her.

Alicia Conrad, Eva's mother Sarah Smythe, Doctor Webb and Eva Smythe Davis were seated in a semi-circle around a chair for Isaac Peterson. Alicia's grandson sat and he faced them. Isaac opened one of the diaries of Grandmother Mary Beth Hamilton. He read:

"Dear Diary,
A few weeks ago, my brother Barnabas and his new wife Alicia, my best friend left for France. They have written that all is well, they're happy and his practice of medicine is getting off to a good

start. Nice, easy to work with doctors in his group. Alicia likes their wives.

The second season has been over for some time. Father is still convinced that I need a husband.

It has been so long since I found my love. Too bad he didn't feel as I did. I haven't called it pining for a while now. It still feels like pining, but I don't think of it that way now. I have decided to call these feelings, a survival of the love wars. I lost in a big way. But since only Alicia and Barnabas know about him, I'm not publicly humiliated. Goodnight diary, I shall go pine away, I mean survive another night without my love.

HELLO DIARY! Two weeks since I wrote in you.

What a tale I have for you tonight! I'm so happy. He, my dashingly handsome dark-haired man Loves Me! I can hardly believe it. Today a carriage came with a freight package addressed to me. Father called me to the study, and I was surprised to see the large package. I opened it, with help. It was the most beautiful painting I have ever seen. The one I fell in love with at that gallery in London. The big giant roses in the red lacquer vase stood in front of me. I had loved it at first sight. It had to have been sent by my man! This painting was by the same painter as the portrait of my man. And it had been taken off the wall when Alicia and I had gone back to the gallery. Oh, what a wonderful present. Sent to me by my love.

Father was stunned, Mother was delighted. Father said, "You must send it back. You can't accept such an expensive gift. It must be a very valuable painting. Look, the artist is a famous portraitist. Since this is totally different from his usual works, it's probably priceless. Is there a card? There was no return address on the box."

No card. No return address. But I know in my heart it's from my man. Now I must wait for him to come to me. Please make it soon dear Lord. I have waited a long time for him.

Mother showed me the best place to hang the wonderful picture. It was perfect so she had it hung, and we all enjoyed it.

Dear Diary,

A few more weeks gone by.

The strangest thing happened today. We have enjoyed my painting for over a month now. My heart sings every time I pass it. It's hard to wait. Then a new turn of events. Father got another proposal from the first man to ask for my hand before my coming out season. The one I turned down because he was so old. Can you believe he had the gall to ask again? I guess since I have not married yet he thinks I'll be desperate and jump at the chance now. Father is insisting that I at least meet the man. He has proposed a trip to his home, so I can at least see what I've turned down.

Now that my man has contacted me, how can I go and meet another man? I have no name so I can't tell Father the picture is from my man, and he loves me because he sent me the painting. Without a name to give Father, I have no chance of convincing him I should wait here for the unknown man to show up on our doorstep.

Dear Diary,

I'm exasperated. Father has business with my persistent suitor. He and Mother are going to his home for an overnight stay and want me to go with them. I have refused. They're angry with me. Are they trying to get rid of me? If I was fussy, I might think they were shipping me off to some unknown territory, not caring what happens to me. I'll give them the benefit of the doubt, this time.

I'm pining again. The wonderful painting has arrived and given me hope. Only to be dashed by his long absence. When will he come for me and take me away in his strong arms? Am I kidding myself? Maybe he is just taunting me for some unknown perverse pleasure. If so it's an expensive thrill. Father had the painting evaluated for the insurance. It's valued at an enormous amount. So why would he send it to me if he has no intention of coming for me? That is right, I'm now back on track. He will arrive as sure as I live. Thank you, God.

Dear Diary,

Mother and Father left this morning, without me. They were distraught that I still refuse to meet the man who has asked for my hand in marriage two times now. They don't know that I must wait here for my love to arrive. I dare not tell them. They might think I have gone daft. Especially since I don't even know his name. Could I have gone off my mind and not know it? When I think about it, this is not rational behavior. But my heart believes it to be true.

Dear Diary,

Yesterday my parents left and should have arrived back home today. The carriage came back without them and the driver had a note from Mother for me.

"Father suffered a fall and the doctor here told us he must stay two weeks at least. You must come as quickly as possible. Bring Mrs. Brooker and your personal maid. I'm sorry this is not to your liking, but we need you here. I know the driver has started late and you must wait to start out until morning. That will give the horses a chance to rest before making the journey back here. We love you Mary Beth. Thank you for your obedience, Mother."

Is the whole world conspiring against me? What if my love comes while we are away? But I must go to them. How could I refuse when Father is injured? Mrs. Brooker is excited to go and so is Sonja my personal maid. We will leave in the morning. Tonight, and every night, I will dream of my love and maybe pine a little or continue the love battle.

Dear Diary!

The day was perfect for traveling, bright sunshine, but it wasn't hot, and a slight breeze brought the scent of wildflowers to our nostrils. Mrs. Brooker kept up a lively discussion. We enjoyed ourselves, then a wheel hit a rock and broke, throwing the three of us all over the carriage, which ended up slanting sideways threatening to turn all the way over on that side.

"Miss Mary Beth, are any of you hurt?" The footman peered in at us.

We all checked, and I said. "No, can you get us out?"

"Yes, me and Jake here can do it for sure. You first, Miss, then Mrs. Brooker, then Sonja."

The driver, Jake and the other footman, were indeed able to extricate us from the carriage. Then they set about to change the broken wheel. "Miss Mary Beth, did you know that several years ago, your father made us carry spare wheels and other items that could break down on a trip? It is a godsend that he did. It has saved us much time and money by not having to wait for a wheelwright to make a new one for us. Or pay the high charges when you're in trouble on the road. Not to mention highwaymen who prey on stranded passengers," Jake added as the three men worked.

I told Jake, "Thanks for telling me about Father making sure we were taken care of in this event. I'm glad we didn't have to wait while one of you found someone to fix the carriage. You have all done well." The wheel was fixed, and we were on our way again. We hadn't been delayed very long as the men were good at working together.

Mrs. Brooker pointed out things of interest as we moved along. She made this a pleasant journey. Alicia and I had always enjoyed the special notes of interest she had for us. We wondered how she knew so many things. I wished Alicia were here. On this occasion we shared much laughter. Then Mrs. Brooker pointed out the majestic trees that lined the very wide lane we would travel to reach the house, Willows Vista Estate. The flowers down the lane were planted in such a way that there would be something lovely in bloom all year long. That took a very skilled gardener. The scents were heady and wonderful. Soon a tall white house appeared, many large windows shone in the sun.

Mother had been told of our arrival and she stood on the porch as she waited for us. She hugged me. "Mary Beth. Thank God you have come to us safe. No problems on the road?"

"Just a broken wheel. It was fixed in no time at all."

"You must have been protected by God. An elderly couple was robbed and murdered only this morning along the very road you traveled. I have prayed and worried all day. Mrs. Brooker, glad you're here. You must tell me everything." The two women smiled.

"The master of the house has been called away for a few days. I'm sorry you will have to wait to meet him," Mother said.

I smiled at her. "That will be fine. How is Father doing?"

"He is asleep in a downstairs room. It's easier to care for him there. A small bed was brought in for me too and it's such a nice area for us. The Lord here is so kind and the house is lovely. I like the arrangement of rooms, it's easy to maneuver and find your way around. Don't you love the flowers along the lane? There are other gardens here to explore, too. I would like for us to walk around later. Supper will be served in a short time, so I'll have a maid show you all to your rooms. Mary Beth, when you're ready, come down and see your father."

The maid took me to a huge room with a tall ceiling. It was decorated in white accessories with light creamy green walls, the curtains were set off with the same green a couple of shades darker than the walls. It was love at first sight. It was mine. All mine. I had to tell myself that this was not mine I would get the colors just right and create a room like this for myself. My painting of the roses in the red lacquer vase would be perfect on the wall at the end of the bed where I could see it. Mahogany, my favorite wood, was matched in the wardrobe and dressing table, four poster bed and bedside table that held the large candle. The bench at the end of the bed and the slipper chair were covered in a forest green.

I had to stop my assessment of the room when I spied it. In the center of the dresser among the wonderful perfume bottles was a red lacquer vase with fresh, large roses. Almost the real image of my painting. No, it was just a trick of my mind. Could it be that my man was the very one who I have been avoiding for years? No, it was too bizarre to contemplate. The world must be full of those vases.

I washed up and changed out of my traveling clothes and went down to greet Father. He was sitting in a comfortable chair with his leg propped on a big ottoman.

"Mary Beth, you look so pretty. We were worried about your travel today. Some bad news got to us about a couple. Glad you were safe," Father said.

"Hello, Father, Jake told me how you had prepared our carriage for a breakdown like we experienced and that is why we weren't exposed along the side of the road for a long time. Thank you for your thoughtfulness. How did you hurt your leg?"

"Your mother and I were walking across the lawn when I turned my ankle in a hole. It hurts like the dickens. The doctor gave me some pain pills and said not to walk on it for a couple of weeks. We sent for you and then Mr. Smythe got called away on urgent business. What do you think about the house and grounds here? It could all be yours."

"If it's the best house in the world but comes with the wrong man it's worthless." I reminded him, as I had several times before he came here.

"Daughter, this true love business doesn't always work out. But a contract of marriage with two great households can be a blessing for everyone concerned," he said as he had before.

We talked until suppertime. The maid brought him a tray with good looking food, then led me to the dining room, where Mother and Mrs. Brooker were seated. "Father said he feels good. Mother, you look invigorated. This must be a nice place for you."

"Oh, Mary Beth, It's, a pleasure to be here. Last time I was here was when the current Lord's father lived here. He passed away several years ago."

The evening didn't go by as quickly as the supper, but it was a pleasant time with Father and Mother. Father did slip in how all this could be mine, several times. I ignored him.

I slept well considering the roses in my room. I had dreams of my love who came to me and told me he had loved me always and would be mine forever. I awoke the next morning feeling refreshed with an air of expectation.

My mission this morning was to look for the portrait, breakfast with Mother, visit with Father, roam around the house. This was the formula for my days. I found many lovely things and wonderful rooms. I could be quite happy living here if this really was the home of my beloved but no Portrait was found. Since the weather was nice, we got into the habit of a walk outside. The days went by and we enjoyed our visit here. The bond with Mother, Mrs. Brooker and I flourished.

One day Mother said she used to love to ride but hadn't done it in years.

Mrs. Brooker said, "We can ride tomorrow, I'll arrange it."

Mother shook her head and said, "I didn't bring a riding habit. I never thought of it."

"You're in luck. I have two," Mrs. Brooker said.

Next day we three went riding with our picnic basket. We saw deer and turkey and several other animals. We lunched at a beautiful sparkling brook where the rushing water made burbling sounds.

We watched his carriage come through the lane. It had an elegant gold scroll, any woman would love to ride in this conveyance, yet manly and strong no man riding inside would feel like a fop. We got to the stair just as the coach rolled to a stop. Someone handed us down from our horses to the ground and he alighted from the carriage.

My heart had been straining for the moment I would know for sure. Was this my true love or another? It was he. My wasting away and pining was over. I stood and looked at him. He was more excellent than I remembered. Those blue eyes and black hair, and full lips that seemed to draw me to him.

He stepped over to me. "Hello, Ladies, I'm happy to see you have enjoyed your ride. I watched you come in as I came down the lane." He tipped his hat at Mother. "Mrs. Hamilton," he acknowledged. Then looking at me he said, "And this must be the lovely Miss Mary Beth Hamilton. Let me introduce myself I'm Lord Jonathan Charles Smythe. Pleased to meet you at last. Ladies, allow me to introduce my beloved sister, Mrs. Penelope Smythe Brooker. He reached out and drew her in for a big hug. Good to see you again, Sis."

Mother said, "But you worked for us as a companion and chaperone. How can that be? This is your home?"

Mrs. Brooker said, "Let us go inside and have tea and crumpets and it will all be explained." She smiled and took Mother's arm and they walked in front of His Lordship and me.

"Why didn't you tell me your name?" I asked.

"When did you know it was me?" Jonathan asked.

"When you stepped out of that coach just now. I knew for sure. I suspected when I arrived here and found the red lacquer vase with the big fresh roses in it. I have looked but never saw the portrait. By the date of the artists death I decided it was made of a grandfather, is that right?"

"Yes, everyone always told me how much I looked like him. He was Lord Wilmerth Francis Smythe." Jonathan stopped, turned me toward him and said quietly, "I have loved you a very long time and I want to marry you. May I ask your father for his permission again?"

It felt like my heart stopped, I couldn't breathe. It was like my brain forgot how to bring air in and out. I wanted to kiss him, but my mother and his sister were in front of us. He put his hands on my shoulders and asked, "Are you alright?"

It was all I could do to shake my head yes. When I could breathe, I said, "I loved you from the first moment I saw you. I have loved you without knowing your name or of your feelings for me. When the painting of the 'Roses in Red Lacquer Vase,' arrived addressed to me, I thought it meant that you loved me and would come for me soon. Then the marriage proposal came. How could I go to meet another man when I was waiting for you to come calling any day?"

Mother turned around and said, "Are you coming into the house?"

The warm circle created by him standing in front of me with his hands on my shoulders and his lips so close was broken and we followed them into the house. He offered his arm as a proper gentleman should and I took it. Mrs. Brooker ushered us all into the room Father was using so we could hear the story all at once.

Father said, "What is going on here?" He had

been dozing and heard us moving chairs around in order to talk easily.

Mother said, "We have become part of a conspiracy. Our companion and chaperone is not who we thought she was at all. I would like you to meet Lord Smythe's sister Penelope Brooker. The man our daughter has been pining away for is none other than Lord Smythe himself! Sir, I think you have a lot of explaining to do."

"Yes, Lady Hamilton, I do. It all started years ago. I attended your church one Sunday and saw the most beautiful girl. The problem was she was too young. I left early and didn't greet you.

I saw Mary Beth many times over the ensuing years. She got more beautiful each time I saw her. At some point I realized that I was in love with her and no other woman interested me. One of the times I saw her, I was with my smart sister here and she said, 'Why, Jonathan, you're in love with that girl. Do you know who she is?"

"That's my future wife, Mary Beth Hamilton Smythe," I told her.

She laughed at me, until she saw how serious I was about making her my wife.

Penny said, "If I can ever be of any help in making that dream come true just let me know."

A year later Penelope was married to Mr. Brooker. About six years later she was back home. She was a widow after her husband's death. She read in the newspaper that Mary Beth was to be presented at the Coming Out Ball. Right after she read the article, I made my first marriage proposal and was turned down flat. It came as quite a shock.

I knew her father here liked me and thought he would be favorable to the marriage. After some business we had together, I asked him why I had been turned down. He told me Mary Beth thought twenty-eight was too old and didn't want to wed an old man. That was really a shock to my ego. Did that mean I would never have a chance with her? I was too deeply involved; too smitten by her to let go.

Penny saw what I was going through. "Mary Beth will need a chaperone when they go to the big city. I'll go to her mother and offer my services. As a widow I'll be highly qualified.

Perhaps I can see how the girl thinks and tell you if there is a chance for you." She did just that.

Penny told me where you were going so I could make an appearance. Mary Beth looked at me with something warm that made my heart flip flop, when I saw her at the Hotel Carlton. I thought, she is either mine or it will kill me looking at her. Luckily, I found out that those feelings were normal and were not going to kill me from a heart attack. I popped up all over town. When I was told you were going to the gallery the next day. I sent a servant to bring the two paintings and paid the gallery owner to let me hang them for the day.

Mary Beth saw the Roses first and declared her love for it. Then Alicia saw the portrait. They both thought it was me until they saw the artist and knew the date. He had passed away, so it had to be a distant relative. I removed them that very night from the gallery and returned them home.

I danced with Mary Beth at the ball, but refused

to give her my name. "I think I said something like, I'll tell you when the time is right."

"Then the opportunity to talk to her again came when the girls went to the gardens. It was a perfect day for me. I returned home and waited, mainly to see if Mary Beth would choose any of the suitors who came to call upon her. I was happy when she didn't.

The time for the second season came. I was joyous when she decided not to attend. But then suitors came anyway. I gave her plenty of time to make sure of her feelings. Then I sent the ROSES IN RED LACQUER VASE painting. I thought she would know I loved her.

I waited awhile then sent my second proposal. Thinking by now she would know it was from me. She refused to come with you and meet me. If Mr. Hamilton hadn't injured his foot and needed her here, she would still be at her home not mine."

"Mary Beth told me just now that, 'When the painting arrived, she thought it meant I loved her and would come to get her. So how could she go and meet another man when she was waiting for me. She hadn't confided her feelings and that she didn't know the name of the man she had met in the park to my sister.' I almost lost out because of misunderstanding how these love things work."

Jonathan said. "Mr. Hamilton, I ask again for the hand of your daughter, Mary Beth Hamilton, in marriage."

"Mary Beth, is this what you want?" Father asked.

"Yes, Father, this is the one for me. I told you I

would let you know when it was the right one. He, Lord Jonathan Charles Smythe, is my man."

Chapter 21

Isaac noticed his grandmother rubbing her hands together. There was a little bit of a chill in the air. He addressed Sarah, "Would you like me to put another log on the fire?"

"That would be nice."

He stood, stretched his legs, put the log on then returned to his seat and opened the diary to the next page.

"Dear Diary,

The banns were posted about two months ago. Now we must wait the required ten months more. We have waited so long already but this time will be special as we get to know each other. We have started well with the visiting, spending the day talking and walking and riding horses. It's so good that his sister Penny is a person I already liked and now we can enjoy each other in a new relationship as equals and friends.

Mother is humming and Father is happy. I'm happy.

Dear Diary,

The wedding was like a fairytale. All the work to put a wedding together is amazing. Shopping for materials, dressmaking and fittings. Mother, Mrs. Roberts, Penny and I went to London again and had a great shopping spree. We went to the gallery where the two paintings hung for a day. I asked to speak to the owner, Mr. Eldon. He invited us into his salon for important customers. After introductions, we had tea with him. He asked me, "Did you ever find out about the paintings of the flowers and the man who paid me to hang them?"

"That's why we came here today, to tell you I found him, and we are getting married in a few more months."

"I'm delighted for you. Tell me how you found him," he said.

I said, "The man in the picture was his great grandfather, Lord Wilmerth Francis Smythe. Mrs. Penelope Smythe Brooker. Here, I put my hand on Penny's. "is the sister of the man who paid you to hang the paintings. When she told him we would be going to your gallery the next day, he had both paintings brought up from his home."

I took a sip or two of my tea and he refilled my cup.

"Please continue."

"I had turned down Lord Smythe's proposal of marriage because I thought he would be too old. I had never seen him. My season came up and Mrs. Brooker placed herself in our employ as my companion and chaperone. She let him know where my best friend Alicia, and I would be going. He showed up. The instant I saw him, it was love. He just showed up where we were each time. One time he was sitting behind Mother and she caught me as I started to wave back. She didn't turn around. If she had, a lot of time could have been saved as she and Father knew him."

I sipped at the tea then said, "But we kept up the game. At the gallery that day I was looking at the painting ROSES IN RED LACQUER VASE and fell in love with it. Then Alicia turned and tugged at my arm until I turned to see what she wanted to show me. The painting of the man we have seen all over town. It was a shock to see it, and wonderful at the same time."

I had to have more tea before continuing. "At the Coming Out Ball he paid the last two men on my dance card to let him have those dances. We danced and danced. He never told me his name."

One day we went through the famous gardens down the street. He showed up and started talking to the three of us, Mrs. Brooker, Alicia and me. We didn't think it odd that the chaperone let me walk with him in front of her and Alicia. We stopped often and all talked. It all seemed natural. That was the last time I saw him."

"We came to the gallery and found out that you didn't know who he was, that he had paid to hang those two paintings for one day only." I cleared my throat. "Mrs. Brooker let him know whenever a suitor came to call on me. Of course, I had found my man but didn't know his name. Without a name to give, I could tell no one about him.

We returned home. The next round of balls came by and I refused a second season. Still a few suitors showed up. I refused them all. I had decided to be a spinster."

We all laughed.

"Oh, no that would have been a tragedy for a lovely young woman to become a spinster," the gallery owner said, "I'm glad to hear that won't be your fate."

"I am too. But he was the only man I wanted. One day a couple of years after I had first seen him, a large package arrived addressed to me. It was the painting of the ROSES. I knew he loved me and that he would come for me soon."

I drank more tea. "Another proposal came from this Lord Smythe. I refused. My parents went to visit him. I refused to go. Father had an accident and they needed me with them. I had to go to Father and Mother. Mrs. Brooker and a maid made the trip with me. In my bedroom was the RED LACQUER VASE with real, large roses. Lord Smythe was gone for a few days. When he returned, he introduced my family to his sister Mrs. Penelope Brooker. He was surprised that I had refused to come and meet him. He thought I would know who he was by now. I told him. I was waiting at my home for the man who sent the painting'"

Mr. Eldon said "I thank you for coming back to share your story with me. I'm happy it has worked out so well for you both. I have often wondered, why he paid to hang the paintings for such a short time. Just a moment, I'll be right back." When he returned, he handed me a glass box with a rose on it's top. "I want you to have this for a wedding gift. I appreciate you for thinking of me. You have been very kind. I bless you and send my best wishes for a lifetime of happiness."

"It's a beautiful gift, thank you. I'll cherish it." We departed.

Chapter 22

"Dear Diary,

Barnabas and Alicia came from France for the wedding and brought their one-year old, Marsha Joy Hamilton. What a cute child, she is so smart. We have had some good times with all our families together. I have missed them very much.

My bridal gown is the loveliest dress I have ever seen. Alicia's mother still sews like a dream. Samson said, "I feel like it should be me walking you down the aisle like I did with Alicia. You and Barnabas have been part of our family so long. We have had a very special friendship." He hugged me in his big arms, smiled at Father and shook his hand. Then walked down the aisle to his seat beside his wife.

Father stepped over to my side, "Mary Beth, I'm

glad you have such good friends. But I want the honor of giving you, the bride away. I'm the proud father today." He gave me a big hug too. The music started, and we moved in step toward my man, who waited with a big smile on his face. Father lifted my veil and kissed my cheek. I handed my bouquet to my Maid of Honor Alicia, smiled at my Bridesmaid Penny, then Mother and Father. I took the offered hand of Lord Jonathan Smythe. The preacher made the ceremony special. We turned as man and wife and I got that first kiss I had waited so long to receive. The reception was lovely. A time to remember fondly. My husband calls out to me. I'll write again soon, my diary.

Dear Diary,

No one prepared me for my wedding night. Shyness, no man had seen my body before now. I was embarrassed. What if I was not what he expected? I had never compared my body with other women. What if he didn't like what he saw? Maybe we should blow out the candle. Does he want to see me? Do I want to see him? Maybe? I spent a long time in the bathing and dressing area off our room. I finally went to the bedroom.

"Are you frightened?" he asked.

I nodded.

Jonathan said, "I am too. What if you don't like me or intercourse or something?" We drank a little of the wedding wine.

I found out the importance of being a virgin that night. All men expect to be the first man for their wife. She has something to give that she has never paid any specific thought to other than hearing in church that she must remain a virgin. Her virginity is her special gift to her husband.

Once it's gone it can never be regained. The woman feels differently about her body. There has been pain and blood too. Then overwhelming pleasure. You know God has created him just for you. He will be your only one for the rest of your life. That's a special thing also. No one else could ever be better and the security of a lifetime of pleasure with the one you love is a bond you never want to break.

I stretched like a cat the next morning and thought, *"This was well worth our long wait."* My husband pulled me into his arms again. Yes, I'm going to love being married to him.

Dear Diary,

We just had our second anniversary and we await our first child. Another three months to go, and I can hold this baby growing inside me. What a wonderful miracle. We have chosen the name Wilmerth David Smythe, if we have a boy. For a girl we like the name Maria Angelica Smythe. Such exciting times. I'm as big as a house. Alicia's mother says the way I'm carrying my baby means it will be a boy. It goes like this; if the mother carries the baby high it will be a girl and if she carries it low it will be a boy. She has seen that saying hold true over many years.

Our love has grown, and Jonathan looks at me with such tenderness. Our baby has created an even stronger bond. Life is so good. Thank you, God."

Isaac closed the book. They discussed Mary Beth's diary and how they had enjoyed having it to tell her story.

Chapter 23

hey were seated at the evening meal when a messenger arrived with a note for Doctor Webb. When he returned, his face looked grim. He re-seated himself, looked around at everyone, then spoke, "Eva, bad news. The Garver woman has run away. The daughter thought we were being too harsh and didn't lock the door last night. Sometime in the night Pearl left. She had a good start. I think she will come here. I took the liberty of sending for Joseph to come and speak with us. He should be here soon. Let us go ahead and finish our meal. Should we talk to him in the library or salon?" he asked.

"The library would be best." Their happy supper had turned to gloom. Eva looked down and realized she had clutched the Amulet of Safety. She didn't remember reaching for it. They finished eating and moved to the library. Alicia had already excused herself and Katherine had taken her to her room. The butler, Donald, announced Joseph, the land manager. He came in and the Doctor said, "Joseph, please sit down. We want to ask your help with a problem that has arisen. You will remember a few days ago when the Garver girl gave us some trouble and we sent her to the widow woman to live. The widow's daughter left the door unlocked last night and Miss Garver has run away. She had a good start on the searchers, and they haven't found her in their area. I think she will come here if she is able to find it."

"Joseph, what is the best way to handle security?" Eva asked him.

"Miss Eva, I'll post men all around the property and the house. We will alert the area households not to aid her with food and shelter. We have good tracker dogs. I feel we can protect you very well." Joseph sounded confident.

"I'm sure you can," Eva said.

"We don't know how far the Garver woman has come, or if she is coming here. You shouldn't ride Candy until we know what has happened to her," Joseph said.

"Doctor, did anyone let her parents know their daughter is on the loose?" Eva asked.

"Thank you for reminding me. I didn't even think of it; she might go to them. If she does, I feel sorry for her and them. They were shocked at how she looked when they saw her last. She could very well turn on them and do them harm," he said, and wrote out a note to be taken to Mr. and Mrs. Garver.

When Eva rang the bell pull, Donald came and took the note to give one of the boys who ran messages for Amber Manor.

The group readings of Grandmother's diary had ended. She could think of nothing but the whereabouts of Miss Garver. The others were worried in their own way. They continued their walks in the gardens. Her mother and Alicia carried the cut flower baskets and they cut many lovely flowers for various rooms in the house. The two of them sat at a big table and created arrangements for their many vases.

Sometimes, Isaac would read poetry to Eva under the big tree near the gazebo. Those were pleasant times. He read, and she daydreamed about him. Would he be kind? A good lover? Was he interested in her? Would he try to kill her? That last question kept popping up, every time her mind drifted. She must not have been a very good judge of men, to have picked one with such a black heart as William's.

It had been over a week and there was no sign of Miss Garver. Maybe she had gone home with her family and they were hiding her. That would be a parent's first idea, to hide their daughter for her own protection. Maybe she was profoundly lost and would never be seen again. Eva wanted her found so she could go riding and go on with her life and not feel like she was holding her breath.

One morning Eva woke up determined to live her life and not let Miss Garver, her dead husband's mistress, have another minute of her time or thought. She asked Isaac to ride with her. He agreed. She thought he was getting as tired of the lack of freedom as she was, since they couldn't ride their horses. Eva deliberately didn't take a picnic. Nor did they ride the direction she and William always rode. She had been back to the tree and over their paths since his death but not with anyone else. She hoped Grandmother's ghost would come out and talk to her. She didn't.

Isaac and Eva had a nice ride. She didn't suggest they race. They noticed several sentries in different locations. It was a comfort to know they still watched out for Miss Garver.

How could she have feelings for Isaac? She wanted him to hold her hand. She wondered about him as a man. *Your husband just died; how can you feel desire for another man. Desire is shameful. Dear God, am I going mad? Is desire what got Miss Garver in trouble? She gave into her desire and look what happened to her.* Eva must take control and not allow such thoughts to enter her mind.

Alicia was in the morning room the next afternoon. She saw Eva come in and asked her to sit beside her. She did, and they talked about flowers. She stopped and took her hand. "My dear Eva, I know you're troubled but not as much about Miss Garver as one would think. You've dismissed her problem until it must be dealt with later. That's good that you can separate yourself from her dilemma." Alicia was silent a few minutes, then continued. "You have a much deeper struggle. With William's sudden terrible death, you have started to doubt yourself as a woman. How could your judgment be of any value if you chose such an evil man for a husband? Can another man even find you attractive? Have you suddenly become ugly? You know in your mind you look the same and everyone tells you how beautiful you are, but maybe they just cannot see the real you. Let me tell you this, the real you, Eva, is beautiful and competent, confident and strong."

"Will I ever be able to forgive him?" she asked.

"Forgiving William and Miss Garver will be hard, but you will be able to do it. When you're able to forgive, this terrible burden will lift from you. It's well worth the effort you must make in order to let go of the wrongs and forgive," Alicia assured her.

"Right now, you've fretted over feelings of desire for men. The desires that titillate you have the purpose to bring you to the realization that you're the same woman. You're desirable. And you will always be able to control them. Women that live a lifetime with only one man control those feelings all the time. Because you have no doubt about yourself or the man you have married, and you have a desire to please him and have confidence in your self-control, and in the things you share and are proud of each other's accomplishments. Evil comes into it when a person gets puffed up and becomes boastful."

"Alicia, how do you know how I was feeling?" Eva asked.

"I have seen it happen before. Some women never get over the insecurity and seek out the company of a man and sometimes many men for sex. They find no man can fill that hole in your self-esteem, only you and God can fix it. We must believe in ourselves. God made us good and we must see ourselves as he sees us." She paused and tugged on the chain around her neck and pulled it out from under her gown. It was the Emerald of Truth Necklace.

"When this was made for me by our beloved Samson, he put spells on it. Emeralds have certain characteristics. Like truth and showing you true friends, true love and other things. Samson's spells enhanced all the stones natural abilities. That's how I knew about your feelings for men. You no longer have the need to seek out their touch to make you feel good about yourself. Now that you know why you were having those feeling of desire, wanting to be held and comforted, you will be released from this way of thinking." Alicia said.

"I was confused and thought I was going crazy. It didn't seem right to have desires and want a man to hold me, especially so soon after William's death. Thank you. You may never know how much you have helped me. What a relief to know I'm not going crazy. Thank you for showing me the Emerald. It's even more beautiful than described," Eva said.

"Eva, you're welcome. I have hardly shown it to anyone over the years. Your grandmother started wearing hers often and it became quite famous. She didn't tell them about the spells on it but some of the old stories about it and Samson and people dying because of it started circulating again. So, some people started saying she was a witch."

Alicia paused, then continued. "Once she and

Jonathan were at a dance. The man dancing with Mary Beth said, "I bet this little bauble would fetch a pretty penny." He grabbed it in his hand. She said she thought he was going to break the chain and steal it. His hand was badly burned, and he started yelling. "She put a witch's curse on me!"

Jonathan reached them, turned him away from Mary Beth and said very loud. "Any man who touches the bosom of his dance partner and grabs her necklace in his hand like this should be shot, not just burned. Is there a man in the room who does not agree our women should be protected from such an outrage?" The whole room had stopped dancing when the man started his unholy howling. All attention was on them.

He then held the man's hand up, using a painful grip on his wrist, and turned him in a circle so everyone could see the imprint of the globe in his palm and the marks where the chains that surrounded the globe had been. The whole design was there. Jonathan walked him out of the ballroom. It was later told that the man had left the country two days later."

Eva said, "Grandmother sure had a lot happen in her lifetime."

Alicia agreed. "Yes, she was always full of life and confidence. If she couldn't do something, she could always find someone who knew how to do it. When you were born, Eva, she saw that you were going to be like her. Mary Beth was so proud of you."

Chapter 24

month passed with no word about Miss Garver or her fate. The household was back to normal. People still watched out for the runaway, but they didn't maintain guard duty. Isaac Peterson and Eva rode most days. He still read poetry to her in the gazebo. They had invited Isaac and Alicia to continue their stay for a longer visit. Alicia told them about living in France and some of her life stories. Eva's mother Sarah was glad for the company. Eva hadn't realized before how lonely it was for her mother before Alicia came to visit. Mother and Alicia both enjoyed flower-arranging and had other interests in common.

Then more drama came to Amber Manor. Miss Garver's body was found in the Manor pond. The constable and his crew had been there all day. Doctor Webb thought she died sometime the night before. She hadn't been in the water very long. One of the farm hands found her. He was so shaken up he could hardly tell them what had happened. He had gone to Joseph, and had pulled him pointing. When they got to the pond, Joseph saw what it was all about.

Each person was questioned. The constable chose Sarah, Eva, Alicia, Isaac, Doctor Webb and Katherine to question. His men questioned the rest of the Manor. Then he and his men got together and went over what each person had said. Eva had no idea people noticed her movements, her coming and going. She thought she did whatever she wanted, and no one cared. Four of the questioned people knew she had been in the gazebo the night before. She was so glad she had already told the constable that when he questioned her. People she would have thought were in bed long ago were out wandering around too.

It was determined Eva was the most likely to have killed Miss Garver since the recent incident where the deranged girl had attacked her. And since it was speculated that she was a witch, she should be arrested and tried for Pearl Garver's murder. She was totally stunned that they could come to that conclusion. Word got around quickly that, "Mrs. Eva Smythe Davis, who had a husband William die mysteriously a short time ago, has been arrested for the murder of Miss Pearl Garver. It's not known how Miss Garver figured into this, but we will get to the bottom of it all." This is what Eva was told the town crier yelled all over the area.

She guessed she was lucky. Constable Miller

said he was holding her in her own home, so he didn't take her to town where she might be lynched. He sent someone to town to pack his bags and moved into the house, for her comfort and protection and to guard her, to make sure she was available for trial.

He then told cook what he wanted for supper for all of them. She told him, "I already have roast beef, potatoes and gravy with green beans and peach pie, cooked for tonight's meal." He insisted she make a ham, mashed potatoes and gravy, sweet potatoes, stuffing and a pumpkin pie, also.

Martha said she did it because she thought if he got his way it might go easier on Eva.

Katherine put him up in a nice guest room.

Eva thought he chose her to accuse so he could stay at the Manor and eat good food, she told the gathering, as they had started calling their evening group around the fireplace after dinner. "How can anyone believe I would kill that girl?"

No one had any answers, even though they talked several hours about it.

The constable told them the inquest would be held in the parlor at 10:00 A.M. Saturday morning. Twelve people were to attend as an inquest panel. Witnesses would be Miss Garver's parents, Doctor Webb, Doctor Tinley, Miss Pearl Garver's cousin Miss Jane Garver, Joseph Moore, Katherine and Eva.

On Friday, Alicia and Isaac waited for her at the gazebo at their usual afternoon meeting. Her mother sent word that she would be late. Alicia and Isaac looked serious.

Isaac said, "Miss Eva, Grandmother and I have discussed this and think it's a good idea. We want you to wear all three of the talismans tomorrow to the inquest."

Alicia said, "I want you to wear the Amulet of Safety around your neck. You should wear that creamy dress that flows nicely with the long sleeves. I think you wore it a night or two after we arrived. That color and flow of the dress will make the amulet show off spectacularly. I'll adjust the chain on the Emerald of Truth necklace to the correct length to lay above your amulet. On your right hand I want you to wear Barnaba's Ring of Valor. We have never put the three together for their powers, but I feel you will need it. Who could condemn you with Truth, Valor and Safety on your side? What do you think?"

Eva said, "I'm ready to try anything. That sounds like a good plan to me. The amulet saved my life before. I believe the three will prove me innocent, show the truth of the real killer and give me strength to face it all. Thank you for thinking of it. You don't think I need to wear a black dress?"

"No, the cream will show calm and goodness," Alicia said.

When her mother arrived, they told her the plan. "With all that power, I hope your Grandmother's Ghost will show up! Wouldn't that be the best way to convince them of your innocence?" They all said together, "Yes." They began to laugh, which brought the constable.

"I don't see anything funny about murder!" he said, which made it that much funnier.

Chapter 25

Saturday morning.

Twelve matching chairs had been brought from the dining room for the inquest panel. They sat the constable at a small desk that had been moved in from another room, as well as the matching chair for it. At the side of the desk another chair was placed for the witness speaking at the time. They arranged the witness chairs and guests in large rows of comfortable armchairs from various rooms. The room with its creamy walls gave off a feeling of calm. The fireplace was lit, and the windows let in a great amount of morning light. People from the village arrived ahead of time.

"Do they want to make sure I'm hung by noon?" Eva asked Isaac, when he commented on all of them being about thirty minutes early.

He raised his nice eyebrows at her and rolled his

eyes. "Be of good cheer my lady, you have great powers attending you today. The truth will come out. I think it's time for me to walk you down to the inquisition, I mean inquest." He gave her a reassuring hug. "You look stunning and the talismans are attuned to you. Can you feel the energy flowing from each of them?"

"Yes. Do you feel it?" Eva asked.

"Maybe you're a witch and I'm a warlock." He smiled. "I think maybe that will be one of your advantages today. Maybe everyone can feel that special energy."

Isaac took her arm and they slowly walked down the stairs and entered the salon and greeted everyone and seated themselves.

The constable drew himself up to a state of greater importance than they had ever seen from him. He began, "We are here today to hold an inquest into the death of Miss Pearl Garver. She was found in a small pond several hundred yards behind the gazebo here on Amber Manor, in a cow pasture."

"Oh, how awful." cried out her mother.

The constable continued, "We need to establish why Miss Garver died and who killed her. Each of you will be called in turn and we shall discover the truth. I'm going to start by calling Doctor Webb. "Please take the witness seat, doctor."

The doctor sat in the chair.

"Please raise your left hand and put your right hand on the Bible my deputy is holding. Do you solemnly swear to tell the truth, the whole truth and nothing but the truth?"

"I do."

"Doctor please tell us about the condition of the body of William Davis when you saw it."

"What has that got to do with Miss Garver?" the doctor asked.

"Just give the testimony I ask for. Answer all my questions." the Constable said.

"His mouth was contorted into a scream and he looked frightened to death. His horse reared up and tossed him into the trunk of a huge tree."

"How do you know that's what happened?" the constable asked.

"Because, the men who peeled him off the tree trunk said that's what they saw when they got there to help. And that's what the eyewitness said happened," Doctor Webb said.

"So, you don't know anything about what really happened do you doctor?"

"Wait a minute, I have seen much death in my life as a doctor. I have seen this before when someone falls from a horse. So yes, I do know that's what happened," Doctor Webb stated.

"Now, Doctor, tell us about what you found out about Miss Garver's death?"

"One of the farm hands found her in the pond. He went to Mr. Moore the manager and he sent for me. She hadn't been in the pond long. She did drown. I think she fell into the pond and drowned. She had a bruise across her ankle that would be consistent with running into a root and falling. The pond is only about five feet deep. I thought she didn't try to get out and gave up to death. I believe she may have accidentally tripped on a root. We found a good-sized root with scratches that looks like that's what happened. But I think she decided suicide was the answer for her. This young woman has been mentally distraught for a long time now. Some time back she came here and attacked Mrs. Eva Smythe Davis. I had taken her to a friend in another area, to care for her. She ran away about six weeks ago and no one had seen her since. I thought the danger to Mrs. Davis was over. I told you this at the start, so I have no idea why you have charged Mrs. Davis with murder. That's quite a serious charge. You shouldn't expect to be voted back into office when it's found to be death by her own hand on Miss Garver's part."

"That's all doctor," the constable said, then called the next witness. "Miss Jane Garver, the deceased young woman's cousin."

"Miss Garver, would you please tell us about the affair your cousin was having with Mrs. Eva Davis' husband William.

She looked at her friend Eva with a miserable expression on her face. "Pearl was blatant about it, flaunting it in fact. She told me she was going to marry William soon. I told her "He is already married.' She told me, 'Not for long." Jane stopped.

The constable said, "You told your friend Eva that her husband was unfaithful, didn't you?"

"Well yes, we have been friends for a long time. We thought maybe William planned to divorce Eva or that maybe Pearl just said that to see if I would tell Eva," she said.

"Thank you, you're dismissed," he said. "I call my next witness. Mr. Garver, father of the deceased."

Mr. Garver sat in the witness chair.

"Please tell us about Doctor Webb's visit to your house," the constable said.

"He arrived unannounced with that woman." He pointed at Eva. "And told my wife and I a wild tale that our daughter had attacked her. He said our Pearl was in love with Mrs. Davis's husband and that his recent death had unbalanced her mind. They must have had her caged up. They brought her in looking like an old crone. This was not our lovely daughter. We had no idea what they did to her. Then the doctor said I must pay a high price to have a woman care for Pearl, or she would be sent to jail. We have no idea what it was all about."

Then Isaac stood. "Where is the defense attorney? Constable, you're being the prosecutor, but we need defense also to be fair."

"This is an inquest, none is needed here, we are determining whether to go to court." said the Constable.

"I request your permission to plead for the defense. I'm a solicitor." He handed his credentials over for inspection.

The flustered constable ask the inquest panel, "What say you?"

"We should allow him to ask questions." said one of the men. They all agreed with him.

Isaac looked at Eva as if to say, minor victory. Then he turned back to Mr. Garver. "Sir, where has your daughter been the last six weeks since she ran away from the home you were paying for her to stay, remember you're under oath and swore on the

Bible?"

Mr. Garver shifted in his chair with a defeated attitude. "She came to us. We had to take her in. She was our little girl."

"One more question. "Did you pay the caregivers daughter to let her out?"

"Did she tell you?" Mr. Garver said.

"No, sir, you just did. What happened? Did she run from you too?" Isaac asked.

"Yes, she kept saying without William she didn't want to live." He got up and went to his wife and helped her out of the room. They both had tears in their eyes.

"I believe that concludes this hearing. Miss Garver was deranged and incapacitated so when she fell into the water, she allowed herself to drown," Isaac said.

"You wait just a minute. We are not through here. What about Mrs. Eva Smythe Davis' husband William's death? I conclude that she has killed him," the constable stated.

"What proof do you have of that accusation?" Isaac asked.

"Everyone around here knows she is a witch. Miss Garver accused her of killing William. She did it. We can't let her get away with murder."

"Nothing you have said is evidence, only hearsay. Which is the same as local gossip."

"I demand a trial, I'm the authority here, she should be hung for murder and witchcraft."

"What specific witchcraft are you talking about?" Isaac asked.

The constable shouted, "Look at her she has

those witch things on her body. People have been killed by them."

Just then his chair moved upward several feet. The constable was suspended in air, he gripped the chair and tried hard not to fall out onto the floor.

Mary Beth, or, Eva's grandmother's ghost stood in front of all of them. She said, "Constable Robert Miller, it's you who should be hanged, not this innocent young girl. You seek revenge for your grandfather. The green Emerald of Truth has revealed your promise to him, to seek revenge on the Amber Manor family as he died. I see his hand was still burned from when he tried to take my Amulet of Safety. It automatically protects, and he marked himself for life with the image of my necklace."

She looked everyone in that room in the eye to make sure they understood and continued. "This is what happened to William. He tried to kill his wife and the Amulet of Safety kept her from dying. William's horse saw me and reared causing his death and frightened him before he struck the tree. The power of the three items in this room is not from witchcraft but from blessings put on them by Samson who saw what our needs were at the time he made them for us. But misunderstandings came and people find it easier to believe in evil instead of divine help."

The chair hit the floor with a thud. The whole room erupted in talking.

Grandmother Mary Beth talked to me. "Isaac is the true love for you, Eva. His heart shows in the emerald. He has spoken boldly and with courage and valor for you and the Amulet of Safety has brought me here to help you today. These people will remember only that no harm, but something wonderful came from the wearing of the Emerald of Truth, The Ring of Valor and The Amulet of Safety. Alicia on her passing will leave you the Emerald. Isaac shall wear the Ring and you shall continue to always wear the Amulet. When you receive Alicia's Emerald, wear both necklaces as you are today. You're beautiful, like your mother. Tell her I said that Sarah, was the true love for my Wilmerth. I enjoyed her company after he died. I was still mourning all those years later for my Jonathan and she for Wilmerth. We had great companionship. Your friend Katherine will be an always friend, like Alicia was for me.

"Any questions?" she asked

"Yes, how does the magic work?" Eva asked.

She laughed. "For many years, I never wondered how we came to find those precious stones in Samson's mine. Then one day I asked him."

He said, "I was a sailor and found bargains on them in foreign ports. I put them in certain places and showed Barnabas where to place you to find the right ones. Each stone had some natural power that each of you needed. Then I prayed to God for the right blessings to put on them. So many people in the church read about blessings but they don't think they're to be used by them and their families. If you told them it worked by blessings, it's not believed, and you're branded a witch. So, I told you they were spells I put on them. God has been blessing each of you for all your life."

"I would like to speak a minute with Alicia. Have a great wonderful life Eva. I love you. I don't see you needing me again but keep the amulet with you just in case." She gave me a big hug. "Remember to put God's blessings on all your family and friends."

As everyone left, they said. "Thank you, for inviting us to the wonderful party. The food was great and so was the entertainment."

Since no food or entertainment had been shared, we decided it was Grandmother's ghost's blessing on each of them. We found out later that no one in town remembered anything about an inquest. The constable had announced that the Garver girl died by falling in the pond when her ankle caught on a branch that night.

Mother was happy to hear what her mother-in-law had to say about her. She had always felt close to Mary Beth. She was glad they all got to see her ghost and so were they. Alicia said it had revitalized her.

Eva walked to the gazebo with Isaac. "I'm proud that you stood up for me. You were bold and brave."

"It was the ring, he said.

"Oh, no. The ring only brings out and enhances what we already have in our makeup." Grandmother said, "The magic that we are using is God's blessings that he gives us daily. Samson prayed lots of blessings on our behalf, all those years long ago."

"What did your grandmother tell you about me?" Isaac asked.

"What makes you think she mentioned anything about you?" Eva replied.

"Because we were in the room with the Emerald of Truth. I'm sure she would have seen the truth about me," he said.

"What is this mysterious truth?" Eva asked.

"When your time of mourning is over, I would like to court you," Isaac said.

"Courting with what intention?" she asked.

"I think everyone knows you don't court someone unless you would like to marry them. You do know that don't you? What would you think about that plan?" Isaac ask her.

"Oh, that's a plan I like very much. Sorry convention says we must wait until the widow's weeds come off. I want to wear colors again. You know I didn't even think about the fact that I wore the ivory dress right after you came and wore it to the Inquest. We must have a long courtship after the year of mourning. Grandmother said in her diary she had to wait, but the wait was well worth every second."

Alicia stayed at the Manor. Isaac went home to practice his law. They would need to decide where they would live. Eva wanted to stay at Amber Manor and Isaac had his home and law office in the town of Tarkington, just south of Chesterfield. They had time to decide on those things. Love is what mattered. Where you are isn't as important, when you're with your true love. What a special gift Grandmother's ghost has given us. The knowledge that Isaac was her forever man, and she wouldn't have to worry and wonder if he might want to kill her.

Eva woke each morning with a new step knowing she was blessed of God. That her day was better when she blessed each family member and friend. She had the good life. Joy and Peace spread out before her. Eva Smythe Davis, in a few more months would be Eva Smythe Davis Peterson, Mrs. Isaac Peterson.

THE END OF THIS STORY
A NEW ADVENTURE BEGINS FOR EVA

About the Author

Janet Kay Gallagher is grateful for here and now and the blessings she is constantly receiving daily. Her son Ken brings her great joy and happiness. She is blessed with family and many friends. Jan enjoys church and going out to dinner with friends. Her groups are special to her, Red Hats for Jesus, The Jewels Brunch Group, The Quill and Ink Writers, and her Springfield Writers groups: Ozarks Romance Authors, Sleuth's Ink Mystery Writers, and Springfield Writers Guild. Her home is in Marshfield, Missouri.

Watch for new releases from Janet and
find her on Facebook
https://www.facebook.com/janetkay.gallagher

Other Credits

- Janet was privileged to have a poem *Family Reunion*, included in an article by Mary Jo Fresch and David L. Harrison. *Playing with Poetry to Develop Phonemic Awareness* Printed in IRA Essentials, Motivating Readers, Inspiring Teachers. July 2013 issue.
- Sleuth's Ink Mystery Writers Anthology 2019 included a poem and two short stories by Janet Kay Gallagher

Note from the Author

I hope you enjoyed reading Grandmother's Ghost as much as I enjoyed writing it. I'd appreciate it if you'd give it a review.

> Thanks,
> Janet Kay Gallagher